The Silent House by the Sea

AND OTHER STORIES

BRI HERON

Cover art by Tyler Leiweke

Editing by S.E. Reid; http://sereid.com

ISBN- 979-8-9994969-0-4

To my parents, sisters, grandparents, and friends, I wouldn't be where I am without you. Thank you for encouraging me to write, reading my stories, and supporting me along the way. Your support means more than you know.

I'd also like to thank my readers on Substack, my writing community and group for their kind words and giving me the courage to share my writing.

Contents

CHAPTER 1
Nightmares?

When I was younger, I used to suffer from nightmares often. Several times a week, I'd wake up in a cold sweat with goosebumps up and down my entire body. For the most part, I would wake up knowing it was a nightmare, but there was one I wasn't so sure about.

I lived in a room with my sister; we had our beds pressed up against the walls. Our room had our names on the wall in an attempt to give ourselves our own space in the tiny room, despite being only a few feet away from each other.

From my side of the room, my bed was positioned in a way that if the door was cracked, you could see the guest room down the hall. At this point, I was only eight years old, and we had lived in our house for several years. Yet any time I could see the shadow of the guest room at night I got chills, similar to the chills I would get from the nightmare.

In the first nightmare she appeared in, she stayed in the guest room, unmoving. She wore a long, tattered dress with no sleeves that kind of looked like a nightgown. She had crazy, white curly hair that went in every direction; it resembled when you would go to bed with your hair wet. And she would stare at me with her mouth slightly open for hours.

I woke up just thinking it was creepy more than anything, until it kept happening. The next night, she stepped out of the guest room and into the hallway. Each night, she'd creep closer and closer down the hallway until she reached the door of our room. She would never say anything, she would just hover off the ground, yet somehow I could still hear her footsteps as she ventured closer.

Eventually, she was brave enough to actually come into the room and would either lay in bed with me or stare at me with her black eyes. I would wake up in a panic, thrashing around in my bed trying to shake her off of it, but when I would open my eyes, she wasn't there.

This was before she would possess me. Sometimes, she would have her face pressed up against mine, her breath oddly freezing which chilled my body completely. It was then that I felt possessed. In my mind I would be kicking and screaming, begging for my sister to wake up and pull me out of this nightmare. Instead, I would remain unmoving; my limbs felt physically chained to the bed as I lay there helpless.

Since my sister shared the room, there were a few nights when the woman would take turns going back and forth between us. I would turn over and see her hanging over my sister, her long white hair dangling in her face as my sister lay there. The woman mostly bothered me, but once this started happening to my sister, too, we decided to start sleeping in the same bed. We figured that if there was no space in the bed, then the woman couldn't do anything, which we were right about. She would occupy the empty bed, not uttering a word, with a soulless stare. While we were happy that she would leave us alone, it felt like you couldn't sleep with her there. She wouldn't get any closer, but it was unsettling in the sense that you never knew if she would venture over.

I think one of the worst things about the nightmare was that when she possessed me, it was difficult to tell if I was being possessed or if someone was simply lying in bed with me, or sitting on me. When I'd wake up with what felt like a weight on my chest but didn't see anyone, it made me question if my sister and I were just scaring each other when we'd tell each other about our nightmares. But I do know that when it got closer to morning, she would just sway away with a toothless grin as she closed the door back to the guest room.

CHAPTER 2

Lonesome Street

The street I used to live on as a kid was called Lonesome Street. And no, I'm not kidding. I've always wondered if it was named something different before we moved there. I had a running theory that my dad petitioned to rename it once he built our house, but then I realized he wouldn't go through all that trouble.

My dad worked in construction, so building our two-bedroom house was a piece of cake. We lived in a small apartment the next town over, and for a few months during the summer I watched him and his buddies work all day on the house. My dad would buy me a box of popsicles for the week, and I'd sit under the tree for hours, either reading books or drawing.

My dad had been saving for that house for about two years. I didn't mind the apartment, but every night when our neighbors above us would play loud music or stomp around, my dad would tuck me into bed and tell me about how close we were to having a place with no neighbors. He also hated socializing with the neighbors. He'd make a beeline to our place when we were in the hallway, and while he'd give them a curt nod if we saw them in passing, that was all that he'd do, not interested in making conversation with them in the slightest.

And then it finally happened. Move-in day. I don't think I've ever seen such a big smile on his face. Even through the hours of moving our stuff in the blistering sun, sweat pouring down his back (I couldn't really lift a whole lot), he still had a smile plastered on his face the entire time.

When we lived in the apartment, my dad never let me hang anything up on the walls. He didn't want to pay for any damages or waste money, as he'd say. As we were setting down the boxes in my room, I noticed the walls were bare, no color on them whatsoever.

"How come there's no color in here? The rest of the house is painted."

He grunted as he set down a large box and glanced around the room before responding, "Well, I wanted you to design your own room and put whatever you wanted up on the walls. I figured after we bring in the rest of these boxes, we could go to the paint store and pick a color out."

I was about to unpack some stuff from one of my boxes when he stopped me and said, "Don't unbox just yet. We don't want to get paint on your stuff, now do we?"

A few hours later, we were standing in the paint store, perusing the thousands of shades. He was holding a book of colors listing the yellow shades, as that was my favorite color.

"Alright let's see what they got here." He narrowed his eyes as he stared at the colors and rattled out, "Granola, sugar cookie, macaroon, buttermilk, parmesan, shortbread..." He paused for a second and looked down at me, "Why the hell are these paint names so weird?"

I giggled at this, and he asked, "Any you like?"

He showed me the colors and after several minutes of contemplating

I finally landed on the color that I wanted. I giggled again when he requested Macaroon paint to the man behind the counter. He shot me a look before a grin appeared on his face; we watched the paint being mixed together.

Soon, we were walking back towards the car. He was holding both of the cans, and I decided I wanted to carry one, too.

“Why can’t I carry one?”

“It’s too heavy for you, honey.”

“But you haven’t let me try.” I was very stubborn and wanted to try things myself, even when most of the time I couldn’t do them.

He set the paint can down on the pavement in the parking lot. I surely gave him a shit-eating grin and pulled with all my might. I moved the can a little but couldn’t get it off the ground. He pursed his lips together and had a slight smile on his face. “Mhmm, told you.”

We set a tarp down when we got home to avoid stains on the carpet, and I asked if I could help with the painting.

He raised his eyebrows at this. “You want to help?

“Well yeah, it is my room.”

“Can’t argue with that. Go ahead and grab a brush.” He gave me a quick tutorial, and it took us nearly two days, considering we unpacked the other boxes at the same time. My dad was a messy painter, so it was a good idea to put that tarp down; he had paint all over his shirt and pants, but we were finally done. As soon as the paint dried, my dad took me to the store to buy some decorations. He pushed the cart as I put in decorations and posters, and finally the house was complete.

The house felt like home immediately. I could tell my dad felt the same way, and soon we fell into a routine. The town we used to live in was enormous, and it would take us forever to get across town. But with living on Lonesome Street, we could get anywhere in this town quickly. The grocery store was literally only a few blocks from us, and on Sunday mornings we'd head over there. I'd ride my bike while he'd walk along beside me. We never really needed to buy much as most of it could fit in my basket, but every once in a while he'd have to carry some.

Throughout the week, I'd of course go to school while he worked, and his sister would watch me until he got home. With his job, it usually wasn't until nearly eight o'clock, but he'd help me finish any remaining homework I had, eat the dinner his sister made, and then he would tuck me into bed. Then we'd repeat that until Friday.

Now, on Fridays, we had movie nights. He'd let me pick a movie or two and he'd make us popcorn and we'd sprawl out on the couch for hours. Most of the time we would both fall asleep, but I always looked forward to seeing how long we could stay awake.

On Saturdays, we usually spent the day outside. My dad would have a project to work on while I played outside. I loved our routine and I think my dad did, too. It was quiet, just the way he liked it, and he always came back home with a smile on his face, despite the ever-growing bags under his eyes.

But that was until the new neighbors came. Well, they weren't neighbors yet; they were just checking out the land before building a house. It was a Friday evening, and we were watching a movie when we heard a car outside. We never usually had cars on our street, so my dad paused the movie and got up to investigate. My dad was being nosey and stared at them through the shades. He said their car was parked not too far away from our house, and they were walking down the street.

"What do you think they're doing?" he whispered.

"I'm not sure...why are we whispering?" I replied.

"I don't know." He headed towards the door. "Stay in here."

"Why?"

"Because I said so." He opened the front door and walked outside and yelled out, "Can I help you with something? Are you lost?"

The door was cracked so I peeked my head out, wanting to eavesdrop.

The woman turned around, her hand on her chest, certainly startled from my dad's booming voice.

"Hi there!" She greeted as my dad walked closer to them. "I'm Jill and this is Mike, we're newlyweds." Her husband shook my dad's hand.

"I'm Lucas, and congratulations."

"Thanks! I take it you live in that house there? With your daughter?" At this point I was standing outside the door, my cheeks flared red as I realized I was caught.

My dad waved me over, and as I reached them, he said, "This is my daughter, Riley. And yes, we do. I finished building about a month ago."

She raised her eyebrows at this. "You built that? It's gorgeous. Are you available to build ours?"

My dad took in a big breath and reached for my hand and grabbed it tightly. She saw my dad's hesitation and said, "I'm just joking. We've got builders."

"So what other properties are you looking at?"

"Just this one." Jill beamed at my dad, and he looked taken back at this. I knew he was silently hoping that they wouldn't choose this place.

Only a week ago, my dad and I had a conversation about how he never wanted anyone else to live on this street, and how he'd drive people away that would try.

"How would you do that?" I giggled.

"Well..." He tilted his head to the side. "I'd tell them there's a bad bug problem or maybe mice."

"Are you really gonna say that?"

"I sure will. You like it just me and you here, right? No loud neighbors, no traffic, and you get to play on the other lots, too?" He poked my side playfully and I laughed again.

"Yeah, I do like it."

"Good, only the two of us should live on Lonesome Street."

So, I was expecting my dad to rattle out those "problems" with living on this street to Jill but instead he replied, "Well, I work in construction, so I know there are a couple of great properties where you could build a house. There are a few open lots on Wilber Street, Miller Road, and..." he racked his brain before saying, "Jackson Street."

"Oh, thank you! We will be sure to look into those," she replied. The quiet husband thanked my dad, and they left a few minutes later.

I swung my dad's arm back and forth as we walked back to the house. "How come you didn't talk about the bugs and mice?"

"Figured we'd have a better chance of being the only house on this street if I listed off some better streets, more populated ones. With how talkative she is, she wouldn't last too long if we were her only neighbors."

Well, he was wrong. Apparently, those other streets weren't up to their liking, as their house started being built almost two months later. My dad was peeping through the blinds when he heard a noise outside; he rolled his eyes and muttered under his breath, "Damn it. I should've bought those other properties."

"What is it?" I asked, trying to peek through, but he was blocking my view.

"Looks like we're gonna have neighbors after all. So much for living alone on Lonesome Street." He let out a big sigh and shook his head in disappointment.

"Should we make something for them?"

"Like food?" he replied, and I nodded.

"Well, you typically make a housewarming gift when they're moved in, and from the looks of it, that'll be a while." He walked over towards the kitchen. "They probably wouldn't want my food anyway."

I shook my head, giggling. Frankly, he wasn't the best cook, but he sure tried. He said, "Speaking of food, what do you want for dinner?"

I thought about it for a few seconds, before replying, "Mac 'n' cheese." He face-palmed and let out another long sigh. "Again? I just made that a few days ago."

I simply smiled and he made a large heaping bowl, and we sat down on the couch, watching another movie while eating our mac 'n' cheese. I wondered how long it would be until the neighbor's house would be finished.

A couple of months went by, and throughout the entire building process, my dad was fed up. A week after the building started, Jill dropped by to tell us it would take about six months, but it ended up being about eight. My dad said it was probably because she was too damn picky and had to make the house perfect but all I know is that we were both happy not to hear the constant noises across the street.

The day their moving trucks rolled in was the day we were building my swing set. I had wanted one for a while, but with it being summer my dad was busier than ever. Thankfully, he was able to take this week off to start building it.

We didn't get very far by the time she waltzed over. "Howdy neighbors!" she yelled as she crossed the street over to us. My dad's head hung at this, a loud sigh coming out of his mouth, but with her being so far away she didn't hear it.

"Hi!" I said and she beamed at me.

"Moving in, I take it?" My dad asked, and she nodded.

"Yep," she said, "I'm not much of a help with carrying boxes so I thought I'd come by and see what you both were up to."

"We're making a swing set." I said, and her eyes widened as she took in our progress.

"Oh wow, it looks like it's starting to shape up!"

"Honey..." my dad said to me. "Why don't you go inside and get that gift for Jill?"

I ran inside quickly and brought it out and handed it to her. It wasn't much, as my dad said, just a bottle of wine and some store-bought cookies, but she acted like it was the best gift she had ever received.

"You didn't have to do this..."

"It was no trouble," my dad replied, but it actually was a *lot* of trouble because my dad had no clue what to get. About two days earlier, my dad noticed that construction was wrapping up, so he thought we should head to the store and get them something as a housewarming gift. We probably went down every aisle until he asked someone, and they suggested a bottle of wine and a homemade dessert. Like I mentioned earlier, my dad's not much of a cook, and certainly not a baker, so store-bought cookies were the next best option.

After that, she decided to join her husband and help him with the boxes. She told us that her husband wouldn't know where to put anything, so she needed to do damage control because he probably already messed something up. She then followed that up with this: once their place was settled, they'd invite us over for dinner. When she said it, I glanced over at my dad and saw the fakest smile I've ever seen on him as he gave a curt nod.

When we went inside, he practically slammed the door and said, "Of all the neighbors we could get, we had to get the most talkative ones."

"At least she's nice," I said. His hands were on his head, pulling at the greying hair as he did when he was stressed, and pacing around the living room. If you couldn't tell by now my dad has never been a social guy. If he's forced to small talk he will, but after my mom passed away, he withdrew from the world. For as long as I could remember it had only been us two; my dad's sister obviously came over, and sometimes my dad's closest (and maybe only) friend, Jimmy, would come over. But it was always just us, and now his vision had shattered. I'm not sure why he was always so adamant on it just being us two, but I had never seen him this upset before.

"It's still us two here, now we've just got some neighbors, Dad. It's not the worst thing in the world."

He let go of his hair, the wrinkles in his forehead smoothing out as he stared at me. "I know, I'm sorry, I'm being ridiculous." He started to have a better attitude about it once she started bringing over cupcakes and brownies. But he didn't like unannounced guests, whatsoever. Jill would come by randomly, and would stand around talking in our living room for over an hour. While it helped that she'd bring over some sort of dessert, my dad would hold back his tongue throughout the whole conversation, anxious to have the unnecessary small talk end.

Once, as she was halfway out the door, she said, "Mike and I need to have you both over for dinner. How about Tuesday?"

My dad's eyes flicked over towards me, quickly mulling it over before he said, "Sure, that would be great. What time?"

"Seven?"

"That works for us."

Dad leaned on the door as she left, a smirk on his face as he said, "Guess I'm gonna have to get used to this."

Tuesday eventually rolled around, and it was nearing thirty minutes till dinner when my dad walked into my room.

"I guess we should dress nice, shouldn't we?" My dad had on a stained shirt and muddy jeans. He had just come straight from work and seemed stressed over this dinner. He glanced down at the dirt all over his arms and said, "A shower would be a good idea, too." I agreed and put on my yellow dress. A few minutes later he called me into his room, struggling to pick what shirt to wear. He ended up wearing one of his plaid shirts and he grabbed a bottle of wine off the counter and said, "Can't go empty-handed."

He shut our front door and linked arms with me as we walked over.

"You look beautiful, honey." I smiled at him, and he knocked on the door. Unsurprisingly, Jill was her upbeat, happy self.

Jill wasted no time to jump into a conversation as soon as we sat down at the kitchen table. "You know, I've never asked you why you all moved here."

My dad cleared his throat. "It was quiet, no one else was here."

"Guess we ruined those plans, now didn't we?"

Instead of replying, my dad just shoveled another fork full of food in his mouth. While he was warming up to her, there were moments where she annoyed him more than anything.

"What grade are you in now, Riley?"

"Third grade."

"Oh, wow! What are you learning about?"

We stayed there for a few more hours, chatting about random things, and Mike and my dad finally found a topic they both liked: hockey. They dove deep into the team and players they liked while Jill boxed up some cookies.

"Glad that Mike and your dad finally found something in common."

"Me too, he never talked to anyone when we lived in the apartment."

"He didn't get along with anyone?" She raised her eyebrows at this.

I shook my head. "Not really, although he didn't really try, like he has been here." A smile grew on Jill's face at this. A few minutes later, we left. The cicadas were roaring as we stepped outside, and my dad grabbed onto my hand even though there were obviously no cars coming.

"See, that wasn't so bad, now was it?" I joked.

"Would've been better if Jill gave us some of those chocolate chip cookies."

I lifted up the container she gave me, and he grabbed it from my hands and popped one in his mouth. "Okay, now it was better."

Soon after that, we began having weekly Tuesday dinners. They were mainly at Jill's house, except for one time. My dad felt bad that Jill was always making these extravagant dinners while we'd bring over bottles of wine. Surprisingly, one night he offered to have dinner at our house. As soon as I got home from school, I helped him clean the house and then he began cooking. To simply put it, he overcooked most things. I could tell Jill and Mike were trying to be nice and eat it, but soon after my dad ordered pizza.

From then on, we ate over at Jill's. For the first couple of weeks, he'd gripe about going over there, and then he'd actually have to drag *me* over sometimes. It took a while, but I think my dad started to enjoy having neighbors.

Then, the Millers came. They were "rowdy" kids as my dad put it. When the builders started construction, my dad peeked through the windows and saw the plot they chose for the house was a couple lots down from Jill and Mike's.

There was no question that my dad was annoyed with getting more neighbors, but every once in a while, it seemed like Jill and Mike weren't too fond of the idea either. When we'd go over to dinner they'd complain about the constant noise from the construction and how they liked having just our two houses on this big street. I started to think my dad rubbed off on them, as that seemed to be the main topic of conversation at our Tuesday night dinners.

After what felt like an eternity, construction finally ended, and the family moved in. But I think we all would've rather heard construction any day than those two teenage boys. They always blasted music as they drove down the street--entirely too fast--and they attempt to hold parties when their parents left town, but my dad would shut that down fast. My dad almost reverted right back to his unsocial recluse self, but thankfully, Jill and Mike didn't like them either, so that gave us plenty to talk about.

Eventually, we got used to the Millers, as the teenage boys calmed down and the street was back to its usual quiet self. But, as you guessed it, another family moved in. Luckily, they were a stark contrast to the Miller family. This family was a single mom and her little boy who looked to be no older than six years old.

One Saturday afternoon, my dad and I were outside. He was building a firepit while the mom and her son had just got back from grocery shopping. They moved in a week prior, and by the looks of her overstuffed garage, they were still deep in unpacking. Jill saw us outside and walked over, holding a plate of cookies.

"Hey, Jill." My dad said, as he wiped some sweat off his face and rose to his feet.

"Hi, Lucas. I see you're finally getting started on the firepit." To be fair, he had been saying that he'd build this firepit for nearly a year now. My dad shook his head with a smile.

"Yes, finally got around to it."

Jill stared back at our new neighbor's house before redirecting her attention back to us. "I wanted to give her a few days before bombarding her, but I think it's been long enough now. Want to come with me?"

"You think we should all go over at once? Don't you think that would be overwhelming?"

"She'll be fine. Besides, would you ever go and actually introduce yourself?" Jill remarked, fully aware my dad wouldn't. "Come on, it'll just be for a few minutes."

We all trudged over there; it was a hot summer day, so we were all a little sweaty by the time we got there. She was filling up a little pool for her son as we walked up her driveway.

"Oh, hello!" she said. She handed the hose to her son to fill up the remainder of the pool before saying to him, "Don't overfill it, okay?"

"Hi! I'm Jill and we wanted to welcome you to Lonesome Street!" Jill handed her the plate of cookies and her son immediately snatched one up.

"Thank you for these! I'm Lena, and this is Carson." The pool was full at this point, so she excused herself and turned the hose off. Carson jumped in but not without eating another cookie first.

"Sorry about that. Is this your husband and daughter?"

"Oh no, I live a couple houses down with my husband, Mike. But they live across the street from me." Jill glanced towards my dad, raising her eyebrows to signal my dad to introduce us.

His face flashed red for a second, although I couldn't tell if that was because of the blistering sun, before he said, "I'm Lucas, and this is my daughter, Riley."

"They were actually the first house on the street here. He built it himself."

"Oh really?" She glanced back at her house. "I have a few projects I need to complete around the house. I was gonna ask my ex-husband to help but maybe I could ask you?" She flashed a small smile and my dad stood there silent.

Luckily, Jill came to his rescue by saying, "He would love to. He's constantly building something new or fixing something. He's actually building a firepit right now."

"Well, I'm glad to hear that. I'll be taking you up on that offer soon if that's okay?"

My dad nodded, seemingly unable to speak a single word.

Lena said, "Thanks again for the cookies, Carson clearly likes them."

"Of course, don't be a stranger!" Jill replied.

My dad looked relieved when we stepped into the road and off her driveway. "I've never seen you clam up like that, Lucas." Jill nudged my dad in the side.

"I didn't clam up."

"Oh please, you could barely get a few words out. Looks like Riley and I have our next mission, don't we sweetie?" I nodded with excitement while my dad looked less enthused.

"And what's that?" My dad asked.

"You'll see." She winked, before heading back to her own house.

A week later, we were outside again. Dad was finishing up the fire pit while I was reading under the tree shade with Jill. Mike was out of town often, so most of the time Jill ended up hanging out at our house. She attempted to help my dad with the fire pit, but gave up soon after and joined me in the shade.

I had just finished my book when I noticed Lena walking up.

"Hey, guys." She tucked some loose hair behind her ear, looking timid. My dad's head whipped around at the sound of her voice. "Hope I'm not interrupting anything."

"Not at all, need help with something?" my dad asked.

"Actually Lucas, I was wondering if you could help me fix something back at my house?"

"Sure, lead the way."

They headed over to the house and Jill turned to me wide-eyed. "Wonder what that's all about." I shrugged my shoulders and we anxiously stared at her front door to watch my dad leave. After a couple of minutes, the door opened and they both stepped out.

"Oh wait, she's coming back?" Jill whispered, despite them not even being remotely close to hearing us.

"I'll probably finish it later day, just putting the finishing touches on it," my dad explained to Lena as they approached the firepit.

"Are you wanting a firepit too, Lena?" Jill asked.

"Oh no, I was curious to see if Lucas had finished it," Lena said. "I'm still amazed that he was able to build this house."

Dad rubbed the back of his neck, a smile on his face. Lena lingered around for a second, an awkward silence looming over us.

"What was that, Riley?" Jill said. I narrowed my eyes at her, confusion surely written all over my features as she added, "You want me to show you my garden?"

I nodded despite still being confused.

Jill turned to my Dad and Lena. "We'll leave you guys to it."

Jill ushered me over to her yard, leaving Dad and Lena behind.

"Why are you showing me your garden?" I asked, staring at her "garden" which consisted of two half-dead blueberry plants and a half-opened bag of soil.

She gave me a dead-panned look and said, "I'm not actually showing you my garden, it's pretty pitiful. Look, I think Lena wanted your dad to ask her out, so by us leaving it might make him do it. Plus, this angle gives us a good opportunity to spy on them." I looked over at them, and my dad was standing stiffly and had a red blush on his cheeks.

"Do you see how red his face is?" Jill laughed. I grinned; I hadn't seen him this happy in a while.

"He hasn't dated anyone since Mom died." I heard her gasp upon hearing this. My dad rarely talks about my mom, and never in front of anyone else. Jill has never asked, although I know she was curious about it.

A few minutes later, Lena left, and my dad motioned us over.

"Nice move back there, Jill." My dad chuckled.

"How'd it go, Lucas?" Jill asked, a coy smile spread wide on her face.

"Good."

"Good? That's all you're gonna say?" She crossed her arms on her chest and looked down at me and bumped my shoulder. I crossed my arms in solidarity, and my dad playfully rolled his eyes.

"Okay fine, we have a date next Thursday."

"Well, would you look at that, Riley?" She beamed down at me before looking back up at my dad. "Guessing you need a babysitter then?"

"If you wouldn't mind."

"Of course I don't."

Thursday rolled around sooner than my dad probably would've liked. As soon as he stepped foot in the house, stress was written all over his face. He was ready an hour before he had to leave, so he paced around the entire house several times. I had never seen him that nervous, or nervous at all really.

"What's wrong, Dad?'

He stopped in the hallway, wiping his sweaty hands on his pants as he sighed. "I just--" He paused, pinching the bridge of his nose. "I just haven't dated since your mom."

"I'm sure she would want you to be happy, Dad."

Tears welled in his eyes as he nodded and choked out, "I know she would."

"Then you better head out." My eyes ticked over towards the clock, and he took a shaky breath in.

"I'll walk you over to Jill's."

At her house, Jill opened the door, "Well hello!"

"Thanks again, Jill," said Dad.

"No need to thank me, Lucas. Now go have fun!" She winked. I gave him a hug before he left, which seemed to calm him down.

During that time, Jill taught me how to make her famous double chocolate chip cookies and I showed her one of my favorite movies. When he came back a few hours later, it was impossible for him to shake the grin off his face. And from then on, they'd go on a date once a week. I didn't mind, because I liked spending time at Jill's. She'd show me a new recipe to bake, and we'd put on a movie while she helped me with my homework.

This routine continued on for a while, and soon after, the rest of the empty lots filled up with families. At first, my dad would've hated seeing all those lots fill up, but he doesn't seem to mind anymore. In fact, he would be the first to introduce himself, and would have block parties at the house.

My dad still lives on Lonesome Street with Lena and their two kids. While the house has some new colors, decorations, and add-ons, it's still home to me. I'm sure that my dad never knew Lonesome Street could be just the opposite.

CHAPTER 3
Script Reader

If you've ever sent a script over to one of the production companies in LA, there's a high chance I've read it. If I had to guess, I've probably read over five hundred scripts since starting this job, and let's just say that I've read jaw-dropping ones and some god-awful ones.

Anyway, that's beside the point. I remember the day I read the script, *Kit*. I was intrigued by it, considering it was my first name, and how the first few pages were absolutely doused in coffee. I was surprised someone sent this in; if it was sent to any other script reader they would've thrown it away due to unprofessionalism. I'll admit, if it didn't have my name on it, it would've ended up in the trash.

Normally a script has the writer's contact information on the cover, but there was nothing but the title. Well... except at the very bottom of the page, in a font so small I could barely read it, were the words, "Installment one of three."

I narrowed my eyes and looked in the box it came in for the other scripts, but it was empty. *I guess I'll just have to wait for the rest.* I flipped open the crumpled coffee-stained page, curious how this script would turn out. I've often said that if a title is boring then I know I won't be interested in the script, but with it being my first name, I was hoping it wouldn't be terrible.

And it certainly didn't disappoint, especially when it started like this:

I was born on a Friday, and I will die on a Friday. My childhood was memorable to say the least, but not in the way that I'd like.

Here's what I remember from my youth: I lived for kickball during recess, I hated my sister, and my overly competitive father single-handedly ruined my family.

I know, I know. Boring, right? Let me explain...

I narrowed my eyes at the limited part of the script I had read. Where the fuck was this going?

If this is another one of those life stories that people always feel like they need to tell, no matter how boring they really are, I'll throw this in the trash. But I couldn't help but wonder what was going to happen, especially if there were more installments after this.

There were a few happy moments in my childhood, and most of those involved kickball at recess. Like I said, my dad was competitive, probably the most competitive person in the world, and I loved that he could never watch me play kickball. I could mess up and I wouldn't have him breathing down my neck, since he was at work. As soon as the bell rang, I'd sprint to the kickball field, ready to be the first one to kick. One day, I couldn't keep up with my legs. I fell and I scraped my knee on the concrete, blood pouring down my leg as I refused to go to the nurse. But I was overruled on that. When I came home with bloodied, bandaged knees my dad was upset. Not because I accidentally hurt myself, but because I was at risk of having to sit out a game or two of soccer as my knees healed.

Before finally settling on soccer, my dad had me outside practicing every sport imaginable. I sucked at nearly all of them except for soccer. Luckily it was my dad's favorite sport but I knew he felt disappointed in the fact that I wasn't better at more.

I narrowed my eyes as I set the script down. I didn't realize how tense my body had become as I read the script. This script sounded exactly like my childhood, but that was surely a coincidence, right? Most parents are competitive and throw themselves into their kid's sports, happy when their kids would elbow others to get the soccer ball, right? I shook my head and dove back into the script.

My parents had my little sister the day of my first big game. My dad was actually in the crowd when he got the call that my mom was in labor. She was at home, not wanting to spend her day outside at nine months pregnant. My dad left the game a few minutes after it started and neither of them saw the three goals I scored.

When I was brought to the hospital room to meet my little sister, I felt no warmth or love for her. Her arrival ruined my day, and I never forgave her for that. And that's how our relationship carried on. While she tried her hardest to play with me or just talk to me, I shut her out. All I focused on was sports...

I set the script down on the coffee table for a second time. My sister, Jay, must've written this to get back at me. She only contacts me when she wants attention, and this must've been her poor attempt at doing so. As we've gotten older, she's made fewer attempts to reconcile with me, but maybe this was an exception. I pulled my phone out of my pocket and called her immediately.

"What?" Jay answered bluntly after a few rings. I hesitated for a second, wondering if this all was worth a drawn-out fight. "You only call if you want something or to bitch at me, so what is it this time?" She huffed, sounding bored of this conversation.

"You seriously had to write a script to get my attention?"

"What the fuck are you talking about, Kit? Why would I do that?"

"I don't know, but this script I'm reading sounds exactly like my life. I'm just wondering why you would write this," I spat, anger filling my veins.

She sighed loudly. "Look I don't have time for this Kit. I didn't write it and I wouldn't waste time writing about your stupid little life either, okay? Someone else must've written it because it sure as hell wasn't me." She hung up, and I was fuming. She always had a way of getting under my skin and today was no exception. But I couldn't help but wonder: if she didn't write it, who did?

I shoved that thought aside and grabbed the script once more, nearing the end of the first installment.

I simply wasn't interested in getting to know her, and neither was my dad. In no uncertain terms, I overheard my dad telling my mom that he wished they had another son; he didn't know what to do with the daughter. My mom would argue with him constantly about how Jay was his child, too, and he shouldn't already be playing favorites simply because he's had more time with me. But he didn't care. He spent his evenings outside with me, helping me practice soccer until the sun went down, despite my mother's cries for him to come inside.

For some reason, my mother decided to have more kids with my dad, and ended up having twin daughters almost two years after Jay. I still remember his face when they both found out the sex of the babies. Of course, my mother was excited, but my father looked disappointed, and that look continued for years to come.

Jay took no interest in soccer, despite my dad's repeated urgings. Like Mom, she knew how to rile him up, and while she was actually a pretty decent player, she quit the team after one season. After that, she decided she wanted to dance, which had my mother's full support and none of my dad's. So, each weekend was spent with my dad at my games and my mom, Jay, and my twin sisters, Molly and Riley, at dance recitals. My family, despite living in the same house, practically lived apart for a few years until the divorce came.

At this point, I was ten years old, and as soon as my dad was presented with the papers, he begged me to stay with him. I agreed, mostly because I truly didn't have much of a relationship with my mother and sisters. Any time my sisters would try to play with me, I'd push them away. And I guess I was too much like my father because my mother didn't have much interest in getting to know me.

Although he was too proud to admit it, I knew the divorce devastated him. It shouldn't have, considering the state of the household, but not long after we moved into a little apartment across town. I called the apartment building the Divorce Complex due to how many single fathers or mothers lived there. I seemed to take care of my dad more than he did me. If he wasn't working late at work, leaving me to fend for myself, he was drinking at home. His interest in my soccer games seemed to be waning, and more often than not, I had to catch a ride with one of the moms in the complex because, luckily, her son was also on my team.

It was an endless stream of going to school, practice, and then finding my dad asleep on the couch with a drink in hand. I did spend a night or two a week with my mom, but it wasn't enough.

That was the end of the first script. I almost threw it in the trash, but at the last minute, I tossed it onto the mountain of papers that I had on my desk. *Who wrote this? This isn't a script, what is this? A monologue of my life, who would take the time to do this, know this about me?*

Jay was out of the picture now, but it had to be someone in my family. There were way too many personal details about my family for this to be written by someone random. I picked up my phone again, knowing I was already on Jay's bad side today; why not add to it a little more?

She picked up after three rings. “God, Kit. What is it now?”

I heard shuffling in the background. “What are you doing?” I asked.

She huffed. “I’m heading out for my ER shift and all of your little calls are going to make me late. Now spit it out before I hang up.”

“If you didn’t write it, then Molly or Riley must’ve,” I accused, and all I was met with was silence.

“Are you still there?”

“Yes, I just thought you were over this shit. No, they didn’t write it.”

“How are you so sure?” I paced around the room.

“Because frankly, you weren’t in their lives much for them to care that much about you.”

I sucked in a breath, but it was because she was right.

“Look I’m not trying to be so blunt and hurt your feelings, but I really doubt they would’ve written something like that. But I can text them before I walk in and let you know, okay?”

“Yeah, thanks.”

She ended the call seconds after. I sat in my apartment for the remainder of the night, wondering who could’ve written this.

I didn’t receive the next script until three days later, after Jay confirmed my younger twin sisters didn’t write it. Those three days were spent checking my mail every few hours to see if it would turn up, and I almost gave up until I saw it sticking out of my mailbox. The presentation of this script was slightly better this time, just a few crumpled papers, but no coffee stains.

The next script was a lot longer than the last one, which made me wonder what could be inside. Over the previous few days, I fantasized about throwing it open and reading the contents, but once it was sitting on my desk, I didn't want to anymore. But my curiosity pushed me over the edge and made me flip to the first page.

I couldn't tell you how long this endless routine was. My dad ended up losing his job after being drunk at work, and he wasn't allowed to attend my soccer games, either, because he always had a drink in his hand or would throw up on the field.

The first time he threw up was during a tournament on a hot July day. I think this was my second game of the day, and I truly didn't expect him to be there. I caught a ride with Billy, a soccer friend in the apartment building, because my dad was still dead asleep after 8 a.m. and I knew he wouldn't be getting up any time soon. He missed the first game, but I saw him stumble up to join the rest of the parents a few minutes before the start of the second.

Billy actually spotted him before I did. "Hey, looks like your dad made it," he whispered to me excitedly, not knowing that I didn't want him there. He, of course, had sunglasses on and was drinking vodka in an unsuspecting water bottle. I walked up to him and asked what he was doing here.

"I'm here for your game, sport. Thought you could use someone cheering you on today." He smiled crookedly and I sighed. I knew under those sunglasses were bloodshot eyes and huge bags.

"Well, Billy's mom does that, so you didn't need to come," I whispered.

"You should have your own mother doing that, not Billy's," he spat. He said this practically every time I had a game, and Mom hadn't attended

a single one. It's like he expected her to show up each time, when we both knew she hadn't the slightest interest in seeing me play.

"It doesn't matter--" I start but my dad interrupted me, slurring.

"Bullshit, it does matter. It's like she forgets she has a son," he practically yelled. Though the irony of his statement wasn't lost on me, considering he hadn't spoken more than a few words to his three daughters in years.

"Kit! The game is about to start!" Billy screamed. I sighed and turned back around to my father.

"Dad, I'm not going to fight about this today, okay? Just be quiet and watch the game," I muttered before heading onto the field.

Throughout the game, I heard his slurred, obnoxious chanting for me. My face was burning for a few reasons: embarrassment and the hot sun. Luckily, with how hot it was, nobody would've known I was embarrassed by him. I had sweat pouring down my eyes and body and was actually happy the game was almost over. We were down by a goal, and I had broken through the defense and was seconds away from shooting the ball, when I heard my dad's excessive grunts from throwing up. I had heard him enough times to be able to distinguish him from others, and it ended up distracting me and causing me to miss the goal completely. As the referee blew the whistle, I tried to shake off the disappointment I could feel from my teammates as we shook the hands of the other team, but it was nearly unbearable. I let my dad get to me and it cost us the tournament. When I grabbed my bag and headed over to the parents' section, I saw other parents trying to help him, which enraged me. Especially since he wouldn't take the water from the other parents; he was still drinking his masked vodka in the water bottle.

When he saw me, he grinned and said, "Better luck next time, buddy."

Instead of responding, I kicked the water bottle out of his hands which somehow actually landed in the puke.

"What the fu--" he started, but I interrupted him this time.

"He didn't puke because of the heat, he puked because he's drunk. He's always drunk. He's drunk at home, at work, and while driving," I screamed, and every parent looked at him with disgust. "I'm going to Mom's."

"It's not her night," he whispered, out of all the things he could've said.

I rolled my eyes and pleaded with Billy's mom to take me over to my mother's house, which she did.

One of the parents called the cops on him since he drove to the game drunk, and he lost his license over it and after that, I stayed at Mom's more.

Tears pricked my eyes as I set the script down. A million thoughts ran through my mind as I got up and paced around the room. That was one of the worst moments that I'd had with my father, and now I was reliving it all over again. The anger I felt back then was resurfacing, but felt stronger than ever.

Was this all the script was? Just reliving parts of my childhood that I was trying to forget? I shook my head and went on a walk, trying to forget the words on those crumpled pages, but my mind circled around them for the two hours I was outside. I knew I shouldn't be this consumed with the script, especially considering I hadn't reviewed many others since I received the first installment. I'd have to pull a few all-nighters to catch up on the work that I had pushed off, but I knew I'd be uneasy until I had the third and last installment in my hands. Maybe the last script wouldn't be all bad? At least that's what I was trying to convince myself. *Maybe the author sprinkled in some good parts of my childhood?* That's what pushed me to continue reading the second one, and would carry me onto the third when it finally arrived.

My relationship with my sisters was strained to say the least. I think Jay has deliberately turned Molly and Riley against me, because of how I treated her a few years ago. I share a room with Jay now that I've moved in, though all I have in here is a bed, because she was living by herself until I came back. She has let me know several times how much she despises me now that we share a room. Molly and Riley seem leery of me, almost as if they think I'm exactly like Dad and have no redeeming qualities.

I try to talk to them, even play dollhouse with them, but all those efforts seem to be in vain. The only times that they let me play with them is after Mom yells at them for being mean to me, which only seems to aggravate them more.

Trust me, I don't want to play dollhouse, but I've been trying to get to know them more, which is more than I can say about my own father.

My dad hasn't even tried to visit me or my sisters at Mom's. I'd receive long, incoherent texts from him about how sorry he was and how he was trying to get sober. But I'm not sure how long that'll last or if I believe him. After a particularly rough hangover, he'd order me to throw away the bottles so he wouldn't be tempted, but after the hangover would subside, I'd find him digging through the trash to drink those bottles. I didn't ever respond to the texts, which I'm sure frustrated him, but I didn't have it in me to care.

I didn't see my dad for nearly two years after the vomiting incident. I wasn't intentionally trying to see him, but my mom, sisters, and I ran into him at the grocery store.

I saw him first. He was in the bread aisle, throwing a loaf of bread into his cart when he looked up at me. My sisters were in front of my mother as she pushed the cart, while I hung out in the back. I locked eyes with him and sped up, hoping he didn't recognize me now that I was older, but I should've known that that wouldn't be the case. He met up with us in the next aisle, his cart screeching on the floor as he sped up.

Molly didn't actually recognize him when he approached us. He had a thick beard now, and a ballcap covering his presumably thinning hair. Although now that he was up close, I couldn't look him in the eye.

"Hey guys, fancy seeing you all here," he muttered, a hand rubbing the back of his neck as an awkward silence ensued. My mom had no interest in talking to him, not even small talk. She gave him a curt nod and moved past him, my three sisters going with her. At this point, he had practically blocked me from moving around him, which I knew was intentional.

"Hey Kit, how have you been? Have you been getting my texts?" he chuckled, his hands now firmly gripping the handle of the cart.

"Yeah, I have--" My words caught in my throat as I looked down at his cart and saw three bottles of vodka. I sighed, anger bubbling up inside me. "But you're still drinking, so I don't want to talk to you."

He glanced down at the cart, cursing under his breath. "Kit, I--"

He kept rambling on as I walked away, not interested in whatever he had to say.

I ran a hand through my hair after finishing this script. At a loss for words, really. I know Jay said she hadn't written it, and I believed her. But I wondered if she truly believed me when I said how scarily accurate this script had been in detailing my childhood. Although I knew she wouldn't like a drop-in visit, I had a feeling she'd make all kinds of excuses for why I couldn't come over if I did give her a heads-up.

Despite living relatively close, only about a half-hour away, we don't get together much. I suppose that's more my fault, as I haven't given her much reason to want to be around me. I knocked on her door, anxiety piling up in me as I waited for her to answer. I almost knocked again when she finally threw the door open, her eyes narrowed as she stared at me.

"So, you're just dropping by now?" Jay asked, a hand on her hip.

"Can I come in, or are you just going to have me stand outside?"

She thought about it for a second. "Well, it is about to rain, would be fun to see you all drenched."

I deadpanned a look, and she opened the door more for me to walk through. I hadn't been over to her house since she moved in, which was probably two years earlier. I helped her move her furniture, but that's because she didn't want to hire anybody and called me instead.

As I sat down on the couch, she brought in a cup of water which I thanked her for. Her eyes dropped to the scripts in my lap, and she sighed.

"God, Kit. Are we still on this? Seems like there is no other reason you'd come to see me than these damn scripts."

"I wanted to see you regardless, but I also need you to look at these."

"Okay, I'll look at them." She grabbed the two scripts and began reading for the next thirty minutes, skimming the words on the pages quickly. The only sound in the living room was the pages turning from the scripts; she didn't say anything as she read. She made faces from time to time, and as she reached the end of the second script, her face scrunched before she set the papers down on the coffee table. "What the hell is this?"

"So, you see what I'm saying now?" Some relief flooded through me at this, knowing that I wasn't overreacting.

She sighed and ran a hand through her hair. She stared at the scripts before shaking her head. "Yeah, I do. I guess I didn't realize they were this specific. I remember seeing him in that grocery store." A shiver ran through her at this.

"I have no idea who would write this, Kit," she said. "But I don't have a good feeling about it. Do you think someone is trying to scare you? Intimidate you by recapping some of your childhood memories?"

I shrugged. "I don't know, Jay. But I don't think I should brush it off."

"No, no, I don't think you should either, but I don't know who wrote this or how to find them."

I grabbed the papers from the table and shoved the scripts into my backpack.

"I wish I could give you some answers," she said, as I hung around her door.

"Me too. Guess we're both in the dark." I hugged her before leaving, and when I arrived home later that night, the last installment was already on my doorstep.

My high school graduation was less than memorable. My younger sisters complained the whole time that it was too hot outside, which it was, but there was nothing I could do about that. My dad had been absent from the time in that grocery store. No phone calls or texts, no random run-ins around town. It was like he had vanished... until that day. When I crossed the stage and looked into the crowd, I spotted him first. He was a few rows away from my mom and sisters, dressed in a long-sleeve shirt and black slacks. He appeared to be sweating through his shirt, much like I was in my gown. After hearing the long list of names, I finally reunited with my mom and sisters about an hour later, and as they congratulated me, he walked up.

"Hey, Kit..." My dad said, standing awkwardly beside my mom. She and my sisters left shortly after, leaving me alone with him.

"Why are you here?" I asked, crossing my arms.

"You graduated, Kit. I couldn't miss that."

"But you could miss out on everything else?" I scoffed. At this point my raised voice had drawn some attention so we headed over to his car.

His face was downcast, trying to muster something to smooth over this conversation. "I know you're not going to like this answer, but it was easier for me to stay away from you guys than have you all be disappointed in me."

Before I could get a word in, he continued, "I tried to get sober at least fifteen times and I knew that I shouldn't be around you all until I finally got sober."

"Have you been sober?" I asked reluctantly, not sure if I wanted to know the answer.

"I have, for about two years now." He smiled, clearly proud of himself. I tried to give a smile, but the only thing on my mind was how long it would be until he picked up a drink again.

"That's great, Dad," I finally responded. We talked for a few more minutes before I headed back to my mom's car. After that, he would text or call every now and then, and we'd make plans to meet up and they'd fall through. On the last time we ended up meeting, he relapsed. I guess he didn't think I would be able to pick up on it after not seeing him drunk in so long, but as soon as I saw him waltz up, I noticed. He tried to mask it by asking me a bunch of questions about how my life had been since the last few months that I had seen him, but we both knew that it would be the last time we'd see each other until he cleaned up his act.

And I haven't seen him since.

The script ended there, leaving me with a bunch of questions about my own life. I grabbed my car keys and headed to the last location I wanted to go.

I pulled up to the beat-up house that was only a few streets away from me. I knocked on the door, pressing my ear against it as I heard some faint coughing, but not from the person who answered the door.

"Who are you?" I asked, my eyebrows raised as I took in her scrubs.

"I'm Amber, Dale's nurse." She looked me up and down for a second before realization dawned on her features. "I take it you're Kit?" she asked.

I nodded, and she opened the door to let me inside. I looked around the house; the walls were practically bare, little furniture strewn across the rooms. I stepped into the living room, and the creak of the hardwood floor alerted my dad to my presence.

His face looked gaunt, adding at least ten years to him. His skin was jaundiced, and by the looks of it, his arms and legs were a bit swollen. I stepped into the living room and sat down in the chair next to him. He still hadn't uttered a word since I got there. It was clear he wasn't going to, but I figured that could've been because I was probably the last person he was expecting to show up at his door.

"Did you write them?" I asked, seeing no point in beating around the bush. He swallowed hard, caught off guard with the lack of niceties.

"It's good to see you too, Kit," he chuckled, before a coughing fit interrupted him.

"I'm serious. I need to know, Dad. I don't know who else this could be."

He fostered a small, sad smile. "I was trying to get your attention. Clearly it worked."

"Why didn't you just text me?" I stared at him; an overwhelmingly powerful feeling of sadness flooded my veins. He had been like this for a while, and by the looks of it, he didn't have much time left.

"Based on our last interaction, I didn't think you'd agree to see me. And I didn't want to force you to come see me just because I'm dying."

"Dying of what?" I couldn't help but ask, not that it would make a difference in the slightest.

"Cirrhosis, but that shouldn't be a surprise." He sucked in a big breath, and in an attempt to quit talking about himself, he switched topics. "Did you like the scripts? I heard you're a big hot shot over at that production company you work at."

"Well, they were a little creepy. I thought I had someone stalking me at first. Even blamed it on Jay and the twins."

He sucked in another breath. "Bet Jay didn't like that."

"No, she didn't." I laughed.

"I'm sorry I frightened you with them, but I figured those scripts would be the best way to get in contact with you and own up to all the shitty things I've done to you." His gaze cast towards the floor, unable to meet my eyes.

"You didn't have to do that," I mumbled, tears welling in my eyes at that statement. I knew that must've been hard for him, dredging up all of those painful memories.

"No, I did. I wish I could've been there more for you and your sisters, and I wasn't the father you all deserved. You have no idea how sorry I am for that."

"Well, we can make up for that now with whatever time you have left," I said, grabbing his hand. He squeezed tightly, a tear rolling down his face.

"Really?" he managed to squeak out. I nodded and spent the next several hours with him, catching up.

We had two months together after that, but it was the most impactful two months I've ever had. If I could rewrite the end of his script, it would read; *"For the longest time, I truly thought I'd never forgive him, but all it took was him reaching out in the most unconventional way."*

CHAPTER 4
Rug

I could never keep them straight. A day didn't go by when a guy wasn't clung to her hip, brainwashed into thinking that the two of them were going to last, despite my sister having her eyes on other men.

By the time she was twenty-four, she'd already had nearly twenty boyfriends, all of whom she dated less than three months before she got bored and tossed them aside. I never tried to learn their names, let alone even try to meet them, for that matter.

She always sought out my approval, partly because I had a steady boyfriend of four years and she wanted what I had, but also because she could never figure out who she wanted to be in a relationship with. We were all shocked—especially me—when she finally found someone and brought him home. He had the charm she was looking for, a stable job, and he knew how to be in a long-term relationship.

Despite having just left his wife a few months prior, he forked over the money for an engagement ring quickly. That excited my sister, because the only thing she couldn't hold onto, other than a relationship, was a job. To make up for it, she'd help him get ready for work each morning, which gave her a sense of purpose, since she normally would sprawl out onto the couch for hours on end.

She would wake up before the sun rose to lay out all of his clothes on the chair by their bathroom, grabbing everything down to his pair of socks, underwear, and cufflinks for his wrinkled suit. She would make his side of the bed, fixing the ruffled-up pillow and smoothing out the wrinkles in the sheets so he would be comfortable before going to bed.

He'd get up real early, charging into the bathroom to get ready, before working his usual twelve-hour shifts. He'd step out of the shower and wrap his towel around his waist before eating the waffles she slaved away to make for him, although they were practically burnt most of the time. It was clear he was nice to her and enabled her most of the time, but at least he was kind enough to provide for her ridiculous habits, not complaining in the slightest.

But, one morning, he slipped getting out of the shower. She took the rug from the bathroom floor to wash it, forgetting that he wouldn't be able to see or notice it was gone without his glasses.

Now, before making his waffles that go uneaten, she checks to make sure the rug is there so he won't fall again, scrubbing the tiles vigorously to get rid of the lingering blood stain that still plagues the floor, as though trying to erase what she caused.

CHAPTER 5
Barrels

There were eight of them, all lined up against the barn attached to the aging, unkept house. They were dark blue, I believe. Small enough for two people to carry, but too heavy for one person by themselves. The barrels varied in weight, making some easier to move than others. For the most part, they stayed pressed up against the barn, collecting rainwater and snow throughout the year. But during the summertime, both my grandpa's and my favorite season, he liked to race me on them down his long front yard, claiming there was no better use for them.

He was a reserved man, and lonely, too. After my grandma's sudden passing a few years ago, coincidentally the same week as my mother, he had no desire to live by himself and enlisted my help to keep him company during the long summers. He didn't have any other grandchildren, so my father insisted that I keep him company and shipped me off for weeks on end to a place with slow internet and barely any neighbors.

In many ways, I was a lot like him. When I'd arrive each summer, he would constantly reiterate how much I resembled him, like I hadn't heard it a thousand times before. After being named after the man, I assumed that I must've shared a few similarities with him. We both had dark brown hair, facial stubble; we were lanky, quiet, never wanting to make a fuss. By now, it should be clear that I share quite a few distinctive features with him, although he has since shrunk a few inches and his once-brown hair is now finally greying. Each night after long monologues of comparisons and a few drinks he would grow depressed and tell me that we've both gone through too much hardship in our lives. Retelling the story over and over about how he lost his wife, and I lost my mother, all in a span of a few weeks.

This time, thankfully, I wasn't forced into listening to his dragged-on nightly speech. Instead, I found myself going through the useless junk piled in his house, since he moved into a nursing home less than two weeks prior. While sitting on his couch and doing the occasional yard work wasn't something I looked forward to doing every day, it was much better than watching him go stir-crazy while cooped up in that small room.

He had always liked his independence. He was always cutting wood for his little wood stove burner in his living room, or using his tractor and four-wheeler to clear any dead trees in his backyard. Or during the summers, he would get his crops ready to harvest on his 70-acre land. But those tasks seemed to be the only few things he did to keep himself occupied year long. Much to my grandma's displeasure, he would spend every waking moment outside, no matter how exhausted or sore he was. She had worried about him all the time, to the point where she gave him a flip phone to keep track of him, although the phone hardly seemed to make it into his pocket. With her not there, I could see why he was so quick to leave his independence behind.

I realized I would need more than a few days to go through his stuff, so I walked on his long gravel driveway, with boxes and tape in one hand and trash bags in another. The house definitely needed some fixing up after getting rid of all his stuff, seeing as a lot of the yellow paint had chipped off after years of harsh weather. Illinois weather wasn't predictable, and anyone could see that based on the siding of his house. First, I set aside a few of the things my grandpa wanted to keep but didn't have space for in his room at the nursing home. I had just come from talking to him for a few hours, where he rattled on so much about what he wanted saved that I wasn't sure there would be anything to get rid of. From keeping the majority of my grandma's old clothes, scrapbooks, tablecloths, and the decaying barrels that rested on the side of his barn, he was more sentimental than I gave him credit for.

After setting those items aside, I went to my father's room. It had stayed the same after he graduated high school. There were baseball cards and old magazines still lying on the desk, old clothes falling off the hangers, and about an inch of dust coating every surface; it was all left untouched. My dad never liked me to go in there. This was the longest I had stood in that room without him storming in and yelling at me to get out. But now, looking at the thick layer of dust and random items strewn across the room, I wasn't really sure why I wanted to be in there in the first place. I sighed and ran my hand through my hair, a bit overwhelmed with how I was going to declutter the rest of grandpa's house. I'd pull something out of a closet and more shit would fall on me, and I hadn't even finished a room yet. So, needing some sun exposure and to escape from the cold air conditioning, I moved over to his barn that was close by.

The barn was almost as big as his house. One side housed his four-wheelers, tractors, and dirt bikes, while the other side held random junk like spare parts, flat tires, tools, and finally a few fishing poles that had collected dust over the years. I remember when we used to fish outside most mornings, our hair slicked back from sweat while mosquitoes pricked at our salty skin. We'd wait for hours, our skin becoming tight from staying out in the sun too long. Even though these poles were old and broken, I couldn't bring myself to throw them away. I set the poles to the side and spent the next few hours trashing the majority of the things grandpa had stored in there. I was setting some of the trash outside and was about to walk back to the house when the barrels caught my eye. Looking at them now, chipped, with rust growing on the sides of them, the insignificance of them felt stronger. It amazed me that he kept them all those years, as he was a man who didn't "believe" in holding onto useless things. I didn't really understand why he kept them, as he always complained they were a bitch to move and store. But yet they lay there year after year, never moving from the side of the barn.

I checked my watch and saw that several hours had passed already, so I decided that bouncing back from room to room wasn't going to be the best method anymore. I didn't like working on one thing too long; I'd get bored and not be able to finish it until I did something else. But I figured if I was going to be doing this for several days, I needed to change my approach. So, I went to his office first; it seemed like it would be the easiest room to go through, and it was the smallest in the house. Baby steps.

I plopped down on the old office chair and started pulling out some of the old papers and photo albums shoved into the messy drawers. Seeing as my dad was an only child, the albums mainly contained photos of him. I flipped through the pages quickly; they were just some faded pictures that I'd seen countless times before. My dad was never an open man, but he closed off even more after my mom passed away. So, I decided to do some snooping. I flipped through the photo album for a few minutes, a little disappointed when it didn't contain anything interesting. I set the photo album down and noticed a cream manila folder shoved under a few other notebooks and folders. I pulled it out carefully, flipping the folder open. My eyes scanned the crumpled, faded paper, noticing it was an old news clipping from what appeared to be the 70s. I almost set it aside when I noticed it was a compilation of unsolved murders in the town. My grandpa always said it was a quiet town, with not a lot of action, which is one of the reasons why he and my grandma decided to move there in the first place. I leaned forward and tried to smooth out the paper to get a better look, curious to see why he'd failed to mention this. The news clipping was from 1972, where it detailed the boy's name was Ken.

I narrowed my eyes; he looked familiar. I set the folder to the side and grabbed one of Dad's old photo albums. I scrolled through several pages before landing on a picture of my dad and that boy. I shook my head and kept looking; more and more pictures of them popped up in the book. I diverted back to the clipping, reading on to see that the boy was never found, and after several months of not finding his body, he was presumed dead. I looked closer and saw my dad in the background of the picture, standing by the casket in his suit on the day that I presumed to be Ken's funeral.

I stood up quickly, almost knocking into the piano behind me as I stared at the next few pages. Crumpled up like the other pages were the obituaries of some of my dad's friends from high school and college. All unexplained deaths, all with my dad in the background of the pictures. That partly explained his cold demeanor growing up; he was more familiar with grief and loss than I ever realized. My grandpa had always mentioned that my dad had a difficult childhood, but I didn't think he meant it in this sense. I continued flipping the pages, and I ultimately landed on the last page that made my heart stop. I found the final two obituaries, one for my grandma and one for my mother. *Why would Grandpa store my grandma's and mom's obituaries in this folder?* I slammed the folder shut and set it back on the desk, my mind reeling as I took a few deep breaths. I strode over towards the door and closed it, deciding to sort through another room, needing an escape from this one. I tried to do anything and everything to distract myself from what I just saw, but nothing seemed to stop the nagging questions bouncing around in my head.

I decided to go visit my grandpa the next day; my previous plan to visit him was shot as my eyes were too tired and bloodshot to focus on driving over there. When I woke up the next morning, I originally wanted to ask him, but I decided against it. I wanted to keep what I found to myself in case I found anything else.

His face lit up when I walked through the door, and he stood up and patted me on the back.

"Already done? I knew you were the man for the job." He winked and motioned for me to sit down.

I took a seat and blew out a loud breath. "Far from it. I didn't realize all the shit you guys had in your house until going through it all. Dad's room seems like it hasn't been touched since he left for college."

"Well, that's because it is the same. Your grandma had a hard time with him leaving for college, so she wanted to keep it the way it was. In a way, it helped her cope with her only child growing up."

"So she decided to keep those holes in the walls too?" I chuckled, hoping to make light of the situation, but the grimace on my grandfather's face proved that I made it worse. There were three holes scattered along the walls of my dad's childhood room.

"Your father always had a temper. I'm not sure where he got it from." My grandpa shrugged. He looked over at a picture on his nightstand of a family portrait we had taken just a few months before my mom and grandma's deaths.

"I still don't think I've processed how fast their deaths were. I wish Dad would've told me that Mom was sick instead of finding out after."

"Your dad told you that she was sick?" he asked, and the lines on his face creased even further. I nodded and his lips set in a thin line. "Guess I didn't know much about that either."

"I miss them." Dad wouldn't talk about their deaths, even if I begged him to. He'd tell me to shove the grief down, and after time it would get better. It never did.

"I do, too. Both of them should've had more time."

I nodded in agreement, running my hands on my cargo shorts

before standing up. "Well anyway, a lot of your stuff is in good condition. If you'd like, I could hold a garage sale to get rid of some of it."

"Did you take what you wanted for yourself first?"

"Yeah, I grabbed a few of yours and Dad's old hats, some old jerseys, and records," I replied.

He stood up as well, his legs restless like he was itching to leave, but he stayed silent about it, and instead responded with, "A garage sale might be a good idea then. Donate whatever is left over, I don't need that junk anymore."

I nodded and left a few minutes later. I rushed back home and set up a quick garage sale at the end of his driveway. Within the first few hours, I sold a couple of things, to my surprise, as a majority of his shit didn't seem like stuff others would want. But the main thing I accomplished was getting a weird tan from my tank top. I almost gave up and was going to close up shop before Henry, one of my grandpa's neighbors from down the street, slowly limped up.

"Didn't take your grandfather as a garage sale man." Henry took a large pull of his cigarette, blowing out the smoke to the side before stomping it on the ground.

"Normally he's not, but he said he didn't want all this anymore. Doesn't have much room in the nursing home." I shoved my hands in my pockets.

Henry was always slow to words, and his southern drawl was prominent, even though he had lived in northern Illinois most of his life.

"I'm still surprised that he checked himself in. A few days before he was talking on and on about how he'd never live in a place like that, swore on his last breath." Henry changed the subject, and grabbed onto a lamp, looking at it intently before setting it down and grabbing some of my dad's old onesies. "Your grandmother really liked to hold onto stuff, didn't she?" Henry chuckled. Despite the incessant wrinkles and faded blue color of the onesie, it was still in good shape, much like the other onesies he had already set aside. "It used to bother your grandpa something fierce before he just decided to go along with it. Helps me out though. Now I won't have to buy my new grandbaby some expensive onesies he'll grow out of in a few months anyway," he added.

"I'm not surprised. I've been going through my dad's room, and it still looks the same as it did when he was in high school." I rubbed some of the sweat from the back of my neck as Henry focused his attention back on the old clothes. He grabbed a couple more and threw them on his shoulder as he reached into his pocket and pulled out some cash.

"How's your grandpa doing? I haven't been able to go over there yet."

"Not too bad, still getting used to it over there."

He nodded while I shifted on the heels of my feet, getting a little tired of this conversation before he asked something that sparked my interest. "Your dad around?"

I shook my head. "He's back home, why?"

"Just wondering. I saw him and your grandfather fighting a few days before he got into the nursing home. Looked pretty heated if you ask me." He picked up his hat and placed it on his bald, sweaty head. He paused for a few seconds, and I sighed, talking to him was like waiting for paint to dry, he could never get a sentence out quickly. "Wondered if he had something to do with it. John seemed as able as he'd always been. Just a month ago he was messing around on his four-wheeler and I waved at him from my porch. I was surprised to hear he moved over there," he finally added.

I narrowed my eyes and said, "I'll have to ask him tomorrow about that. Thanks for coming, Henry, and buying some of those clothes."

He waved me off before saying, "No, thank your grandpa for me. This new grandbaby's been growing so fast, he was in need of some new clothes."

Henry left a few minutes later and I remained outside for nearly four hours after, hovering over this little plastic table, roasting in the heat. Thankfully, the majority of the items were bought, leaving only a few items to donate. I packed up the table and placed it in the garage, my skin hot from the burning sun, before I rejoiced at the cool air conditioning that chilled the house. Even though every muscle in my body ached from standing and going through boxes all day, I decided to keep sorting, knowing I wouldn't get through it if I didn't spend more time sifting through everything. It was a little after midnight when I finished. While I should've been sorting, I found myself preoccupied with going through my father's room, the folder, and the photo album in hopes of digging something else up. And when I couldn't find anything else, I laid awake most of the night, trying to decide whether it was worth bringing it up to my grandpa or not.

I woke up early the next morning and groaned over the fact that my car's battery was dead. Grandpa's truck was in the garage, dust collecting on the hood. It was hard to believe the truck got in a fatal accident, killing my grandma, a few years prior. I was surprised the truck could even be fixed, considering most of its parts were discontinued. Thankfully, despite a few sputters, the truck roared to life, and I drove over to grandpa before the sun rose. It felt like I was spending more time at the nursing home and driving than going through shit at his house.

As I walked up, I saw grandpa peeking through his blinds. He gave me a small grin upon noticing his truck.

"Decided to take my truck for a spin today?" he asked, the second I walked in.

"Mine wouldn't start. Despite the dust, your truck looks brand new. Hard to believe it ever got into an accident."

"Well, you never saw it totaled, didn't really need any fixing." Grandpa replied with a harsh tone.

I narrowed my eyes and changed the subject. "Why'd you check in here after Dad visited?"

"I didn't check in after your dad came, why do you think that?"

"Henry seemed to think so," I replied, sitting down in the chair next to him as he stopped rocking his chair.

He rolled his eyes and grunted. "Henry always tries to start shit, jumping to conclusions prematurely."

"Why don't I believe that?" I said. He stared at me, looking like he was biting his tongue, trying to not make this worse.

"I'm not sure what else to say, John. Believe what you want, alright?" he retorted a few minutes later. I rubbed my hands on my pants and stood up to leave before he quipped, "Forgot to mention this earlier, but just leave those old barrels, okay? They're too heavy for a person to move by themselves, so no need to worry yourself with it." I nodded and went back to his house, feeling more annoyed and confused than ever.

I tried to let it escape my mind, but his persistent request to not touch the barrels made me more curious to do so. I didn't tell him this, but he had already reminded me more than a few times not to mess with them. When we'd roll on them when I was a kid, they didn't seem so heavy, so why was he so adamant that they were now?

I stared at the barrels for a few minutes, the sun beating down on my back, before I let my curiosity get the best of me. I grabbed one of the barrels and tried to slide it off the gravel rocks, getting more resistance than I expected. My muscles grew tired after a few minutes of tugging, as all I managed to do was move it a mere few inches. Guess Grandpa was right; they were heavier than I thought they would be. I was about to get it onto the grass when the lid popped off. I jumped back as red-tinged liquid gushed out of it. I rushed over to put the lid back on when I peeked my head inside. My eyes widened and jaw dropped. What appeared to be a thick red substance pooled at the bottom of the barrel, but it had the consistency of blood as I wiped some off of my shoe onto the grass.

Torn fragments of a shirt and jeans were stuck to the side while hair and various body parts floated in the liquid. I took a few steps backward, my legs shaky as I tripped over them and fell to the ground, scuffing my elbows as my heart thumped wildly in my chest. I laid on the ground for a few seconds, trying to catch my breath and prevent myself from throwing up. My head whipped around when I heard the all-too-familiar sound of my dad's muffler on his truck coming up the road. I scrambled up to my feet and slammed the lid onto the barrel before pushing the barrel back into its place. I bent down and wiped some of the red liquid off of my shoe, noticing a small ring glimmering in the sunlight. I grabbed it and quickly shoved it into my pocket before my dad could see.

My sweaty hair flopped into my face as I pushed it back, and I tried to compose myself as my dad was walking towards me. He walked over with his eyes shielded by his hand, trying to adjust to the bright sunlight.

"Hey Dad, what are you doing here?" I asked, trying to keep the trembling in my voice at a minimum so he wouldn't notice.

"I know you've been working hard, so I wanted to check in on ya and see how you were doing," he said, as he rubbed the back of his neck.

"Not bad, but I've only been here for a few days," I replied. I glanced back, noticing the barrels had moved slightly. I whipped my head back towards him, trying not to draw too much attention to them. "Did you visit Grandpa?"

He narrowed his eyes, seeming a little agitated with my short responses. "Just came from there." He pursed his lips and gave me a look over, before stepping to the side of me to stare at the small, red puddle that formed on the dry grass.

"What's that?" He asked, taking a few strides over to it.

"Oh, I just had a nosebleed a few minutes ago. Didn't want to get any blood in the house." I laughed, hoping to divert his attention away.

"Right..." He trailed off and gave me a pointed look. He headed towards his truck and I followed him. He shut the door and rolled down his window, his arm hanging on the door before he added, "I'm gonna head into town for a few hours, so keep working on the house, alright?"

"I'll probably head over to see Grandpa in a few hours."

He nodded and backed out of the driveway, the dust from the gravel making it hard to see his truck leave the road. After his truck was out of my sight, I sprinted inside and grabbed the folder and ring, deciding that I couldn't wait any longer on this.

I stormed into Grandpa's room a few minutes later, my breath labored from sprinting. He was sitting in his rocking chair, his hands grasping the armrests as he leaned forward, about to greet me before I threw down the folder. His face paled instantly, and he raised his shaky hand to grab it. He set the folder and ring on his lap and glanced up at me with tear-filled eyes.

"What's this?" he said, trying to play up his innocence. I huffed and opened the folder for him, seeing red as I pulled out the various news clippings.

I ignored his question and yelled, “Why’d you do that? How could you do that for him?”

“Keep your voice down,” he spat, before loosening his scrunched-up face, the deep wrinkles set into his forehead. He quickly walked over and shut the door. “What are you talking about?”

“You damn well know what I’m talking about,” I seethed.

He dropped the act and whispered, “I need you to calm down and just listen to me, alright?” He sighed, rubbing his temples as he sat forward in his chair. “At first, I thought it was an accident with Ken. Your father always had a temper, going back and forth to the principal’s office, and picking fights with other kids at school. But I truly thought it was an accident. They were playing in the backyard while I was in the shed and your grandma was away at her mother’s house. It’s a small town. Everybody in town would know it was him and he was just a kid at the time, John. Barely nine years old, he didn’t understand what was happening...”

“What did you say to his parents?” I interrupted, my heart racing as I took a few steps back.

“We just said he left to go home and assumed he made it back. But then it kept happening. I promise you that as soon as you were born it wasn’t about protecting him, it was protecting you. I did it all for you.”

“I still don’t understand why you did all of that for him,” I muttered, finding it difficult to look him in the eye.

“I didn’t say I was proud of all the things I did for my son.” His face looked pained, and it rippled as he fought back tears. “Do you think I want to be stuck here? Confined to a tiny room, shitty food, and rude nurses?"

"Did you want me to find out? Is that why you had me clean out your house?" I asked. He grew silent and sank back in his chair, while my mind wandered.

After my grandma and my mom died, both my grandpa and my dad had barely spoken more than a few sentences about them. Neither one of them had a funeral, and in the years since then, I still didn't know how either one of them died. I felt the color drain from my face and felt so lightheaded, like I was going to pass out. My grandpa looked over towards me, my realization dawning on his features as he shakily tried to kneel in front of me. I waved him away and his face fell.

"I never went to their funerals," I whispered, each word hurting me more and more as I continued on. "All this time I thought it was because you were protecting me, but you were really just hiding what he did."

"Your dad was so happy when he met your mom. I thought he'd stop after he met her." He took a big gulp as if the next sentence was too painful for him to say. "And he did, until an argument arose, and he got reckless and let his anger take over. He said he felt remorse, and so I hid her, too. I never realized how serious it was until this, John. You have to believe me."

I stayed silent and he huffed, knowing I wasn't going to give him the satisfaction of believing him. "I was afraid if I didn't help him that it was going to happen to me. We all try to work on ourselves, John. Your father is one of those people. He's trying." His head hung low as he was unable to meet my eyes.

My head whipped towards his direction. "Grandpa, working on yourself is trying to lose weight, drink less, or hell... see a therapist. Killing people isn't working on yourself. Has he been working on himself for the past thirty years? Has he been working on himself after killing his own fucking mother and wife after a fit of rage? He hasn't been working on himself, he's been making excuses and buying himself more time by having you cover it all up."

He exhaled loudly. "I thought that you should know. I didn't want you to get dragged into it like I was." He looked like a weight on his shoulders had been lifted had been there for decades. The wrinkles on his face lessened and he appeared to relax a little easier.

"What are we going to do now?" I asked.

"What do you mean?"

I sighed. "How am I supposed to go back there? He came over a few hours ago and snooped around."

"Did you talk to him about it?"

"No, how could I?" I sat down, feeling lightheaded again before glancing back towards him. "He didn't say anything, but it looked like he noticed the barrels were moved."

His eyes widened. "Have you talked to him since?"

"I keep dodging his questions for the most part, but sooner or later, he's gonna wonder why." I stood up and walked over to the door. I needed to leave and clear my head. I grabbed the handle and threw the door open to walk out before I realized.

"I told him I'd come over here, Grandpa. He just said he had a few errands to run. What makes you think he won't come back here?"

"John, no, wait." He grabbed my arm, his grip firm as he tugged me back slightly. "We need to talk about this more. What if your father put it together, John? What then?"

Heavy footsteps rang outside the hallway, stopping a few feet from the door. My dad slowly walked into the doorway, his body leaning on the frame as his eyes flickered between us.

"What then, John?" His sinister eyes were on display as my breath hitched. I gulped, and the hairs on the back of my neck stood up as my grandpa's face paled for the second time that day.

I shouldn't have gone through Grandpa's house.

CHAPTER 6
C-Section Scar

I can pack all of my belongings and my son's in under thirty minutes. I attribute part of this to my military kid upbringing. My parents liked to live the minimalist lifestyle; they'd only put a few decorations up here and there. And while I hated seeing bare walls on each house or apartment we lived in, I definitely see the appeal now.

My son is homeschooled because it is easier to do that than explain to his teachers why we move so often. And before you ask, it's not because of the military. Granted, my son is only in first grade, so I'm finding the material relatively easy to teach, but I'm sure in a few years it'll get hairy.

My son, Carter, is always a good sport about leaving. He may not fully understand why at times, but he's too young for me to tell the whole story and I don't want to burden him with that right now. This has been the longest we've stayed in one place; it's almost been eight months now. Which I've found is long enough for Carter to make friends, and I love and hate that at the same time. Not at the thought of him making friends, but the inevitable conversation I'm going to have to have with him when the time comes to leave.

He took the last move a little hard, and frankly, I did, too. I moved us to the West Coast, a place I had always wanted to live since I was little but never got the chance to. I wanted Carter to breathe in the saltiness of the seawater, put his feet in the sand, and build sandcastles. I wanted him to experience what it was like to just be a kid for once, and hopefully put down roots. And he got to do that, but only for a measly four weeks.

Now dreary Seattle, a place I never wanted to move to because of its constant gloominess and downpouring rain, is the place we get to call home. Well, at least until she finds us again, and I hope for Carter's sake she won't.

I suppose I should tell you the story of why we are running. On the day that I turned 38, I realized how quickly my biological clock was ticking. I had two failed marriages at that point, and I was desperate to have my own child. I did a few rounds of IVF using a sperm donor, and when I received countless negative pregnancy tests, my hope dwindled, and so did my bank account. I felt hopeless, until my sister volunteered to carry my child for me and be my surrogate.

I was surprised to say the least, considering we had a rocky relationship over the years and rarely saw eye to eye. But when she offered to be my surrogate, it was as though we had a clean slate. Though I'll admit at times that I was jealous that she could be pregnant while I couldn't. But I knew, without her, I wouldn't be having a child. I was just thankful she was doing this for me.

Her labor was horrendous. She pushed and pushed for hours and wanted nothing more than a natural home birth. The home birth was one she planned for as soon as she found out she was pregnant, but instead, she was taken to the hospital for an emergency C-section. I held her hand the entire time throughout the ride in the ambulance and to the surgery.

I felt as though I had taken a breath for the first time when I heard his cry. When he was set in my arms instead of hers, I watched her joyous expression turn to envy.

As she laid in the hospital bed, recovering, she stared at him in the bassinet before turning to me. "Can I name him?"

My eyes flickered towards her, her mouth agape as she gave me a sweet smile. "Name him?" I asked, still in awe.

"Yeah, I had a whole list of names while I was pregnant, and now that I've seen him, I have the perfect name." She paused, waiting for my reaction. I raised my eyebrow and she replied, "Elliot." Excitement was written all over her face as soon as she said it. While I didn't hate the name, I have always wanted to name my son Carter. There were no words to explain how grateful I was that she did this for me, but I couldn't just give up the name that I had been wanting to use for years.

"Carter Elliot Smith." I said. Her face dimmed.

"So, you won't use Elliot as his first name?"

I shook my head, and she plastered on a fake smile, one that I thought was real at the time. "I love it."

When I left to go to the bathroom, I thought I heard her call him Elliot. But I didn't know if I was just being paranoid and hearing things, so I brushed it off.

The first couple of months were hard, way harder than I was expecting. Carter was colicky, barely sleeping, and therefore neither did I. My sister was more than helpful and even started living in my guest room to help with those late-night feeds and anything else I needed. It was perfect, until I woke up one morning and they were gone. It took me almost a week to find them, and that was only because my mom managed to trap them at her house. My mom knew that she was trying to claim him as her own when she called him Elliot.

Now, looking back at it, I wish I never would have taken her up on her offer. Not that I don't love my son, but I don't love having to move every time she discovers where we live. I hoped she would move on by now, but she's reminded of Carter any time she glances down at her C-section scar.

She's been on our tail a few times now, and each time I've managed to escape, put distance between us. I never feel settled wherever we land. Our apartment is at the end of the hallway, and anxiety creeps up on me whenever I hear footsteps in the corridor. I can't help but wonder if those footsteps are hers.

CHAPTER 7
The Silent House by the Sea

I only got to see my dad during the summers. This was after the divorce, and my mom fought for sole custody, but the judge granted him joint custody, and they mutually decided that summer was the best. But, I hated it. A few months after the divorce was finalized my dad decided to move to Maine, said it was a dream of his, so that meant that I spent my summers up in his quiet house.

I never got to spend my summers with my friends, and what made it worse was where my dad lived in Maine. He lived on the coast in a house that had no neighbors and no other kids to hang out with, so that meant I was stuck trying to entertain myself for three months. My dad is what you'd call a recluse, likes to stay indoors and work. He was a writer, and constantly had a new story in mind that seemed to take higher priority than me. Leading up to leaving every summer, my mom would jam-pack our week with fun activities, and she'd cry for days before I left. She'd then angrily rant about how she should've got full custody, seeing as my dad enjoyed working more than interacting with me.

"To this day I still don't understand why he got joint custody." She'd shake her head, angry tears forming in her eyes. "It seems like every summer you're gone, you grow up so much and aren't my little boy anymore, Chance." She'd pout and wrap me up in a super long hug.

To make matters worse is that my dad hated flying, so he'd drive to Mom's house in Tennessee and then we'd spend what felt like an eternity in the car together, listening to boring news stations. Every once in a while, he'd ask me how the past school year was, or if I was into anything new, but it seemed like it was draining for him to be in the car with me. I'm sure it was the driving, but I couldn't help but feel it was me.

As soon as he threw the car in "park" he'd rush inside the house, leaving me alone. He'd retreat to his room, and I'd lounge on the couch watching TV. He also wasn't much of a cook, either, so we relied on either grabbing takeout (which took a while, since town was pretty far away) or he'd make something on the grill like hamburgers or hotdogs, but eating those day after day gets tiring.

One summer, the second day I was there, he actually sat down on the couch with me. He cleared his throat until I took my eyes off the TV and he said, "Do you like arcades?"

The next thing I knew we were standing in front of the town's arcade. According to my dad, this arcade had just opened a few weeks ago, and with how packed it was I could believe it. There's not much entertainment in this town, so we had to wait in line for a bit. When we finally got in, I was overwhelmed with how many machines there were. My dad stood behind me with his hands in his pockets as I scoped out which game I wanted to play first. He stood quiet behind me for a few until I stumbled on the game, Galaga. I hadn't heard of it before, so I turned to him and asked, "Have you ever played?"

My dad perked up at this, a smile wide on his face, before he said, "Of course I have, want me to show ya?"

I nodded and he cracked his knuckles. "Alright, watch this." For the next few moments, I was in awe as I watched him play. He got the high score and turned to me. "Think you can beat that?"

"Probably not."

"Well, go ahead." I stepped forward and began playing, and it's safe to say that I didn't come close, but I loved how excited he was and how much fun he had. Normally he's such a strict and rigid person, and this was one of the few times he had let loose, especially after the divorce.

We played Galaga for nearly an hour, which surely pissed off some people, since we were hogging it, but I didn't care. After a long line formed behind us, we decided to quit, but as I looked back and saw my dad's high score, I had a feeling no one would beat it. When we got home, my dad couldn't stop talking about it, and I finally thought we found something in common.

But I was wrong. The next day he reverted back to his old self. He cooped up in his room all morning, and when he finally came down for lunch, I asked him if he wanted to stop by the arcade again, and he replied, "Got a lot of work to do."

And the rest of the summer was like that. He barely acknowledged me, and it got to the point where I found some friends at the arcade after riding my bike there, which made the summer a lot more bearable.

Soon enough, my mom drove all the way to pick me up at the end of the summer. Typically, kids hate when summer is over, but I couldn't wait. I said my goodbyes to Dad and slammed the door with a huff.

"That bad, huh?" Mom asked.

I simply nodded, not wanting to get into it. Out of the nearly three months I was there, I could count on one hand how many good days we had there together. After I got back home with my mom, Dad and I would talk on the phone for two hours every Sunday to keep in touch. It usually was the same conversation as the week before, and we'd sit in awkward silence as we tried to figure out what else to say. The school year went by quickly and soon enough, another summer rolled around.

While my dad was better at talking to me over the course of the year, I had a feeling that this summer would be the same as the last. He rolled up to our driveway and my mom gave me a long hug.

"Happy school's out?" my dad asked. I shrugged and he took off, embarking on our long drive. I was determined to make this summer better than the last one, so I tried to be more open and talk more.

"So, anything new open up in town?" I asked.

He mulled it over for a minute before shaking his head.

I sighed. "Arcade still open?"

Again he shook his head, and I dropped it, upset my backup plan of the arcade was now ruined. We talked here and there, but it was mostly me just listening to my music, taking in the scenery.

Once he pulled into the town, I scanned to see if there was anything I could try to convince my dad to do. *Looks like a comic bookstore replaced the arcade, so I might be able to drag him to that.* There also was a new indoor go-cart place, which shocked me, seeing as this town only had one gas station. I was happy I could at least find something to do, hopefully.

Unsurprisingly, as soon as we stepped foot into the house, he took off to his room again, shutting himself away. I let it go, not wanting to pick a fight. But tomorrow I was going to make sure we'd start the summer off on a good note.

When he came down the stairs that next morning, I was already eating cereal at the counter, and he gave me a curt smile before pouring himself a bowl.

"So, what are we going to do today, Dad?" I asked.

"Well, I've got some things to work on."

I rolled my eyes and ate another spoonful of cereal.

"Don't roll your eyes," he scolded while I scoffed, forgetting how much he hated when I did that.

I set my spoon down and replied, "Is this how it's gonna be this summer?"

He narrowed his eyes. "What do you mean?"

"All you've done every summer is work and lock yourself up in that room. What are you even working on, anyway?" His face lit up with excitement upon my asking, ignoring the workaholic comment.

"I've been writing stories, compiling them into a book. You know, I think you'll like them. They're little adventures. Why don't I grab one of them and you can tell me what you think?"

"Can I do that later?"

He looked a little disappointed, but shook it off. "Sure, how about I finish up this latest story--"

I sighed, crossing my hands across my chest before he took the hint. "I suppose I can set work aside today; did you have anything in mind to do?"

"What about that go-cart place?"

His eyes widened at this. “You really want to go there?” I nodded, and he rubbed his forehead before mumbling, “Alright, let’s go then.”

Throughout the whole drive, he was not-so-subtly trying to talk me out of the go-cart place, and to go somewhere else instead. We stood in front of the doors, and my dad stood in his typical stance of his hands in his pockets as he stared at the lit-up sign. It was a miracle I dragged him there in the first place, so I was hoping he wouldn’t get hurt.

The instructor walked us through how to operate the go-carts, and soon enough we were off racing around the course. I didn’t expect Dad to have so much fun, and it felt like we were playing Mario Kart around the track. We did a couple of laps before another group joined behind us, and one of them accidentally ran into my dad really hard. My dad lost control and hit a wall before coming to an abrupt stop. I quickly got out of my cart and ran over to him, as did the instructors.

He grunted as he took off his helmet and placed it on the ground as the instructor asked, “Are you okay, sir?”

He grunted once more as he tried to move. “I will be, can you help me out of this?”

The instructor slowly pulled him out, but not without my dad cussing up a storm. He sat down on a bench and winced.

“Do you want me to call an ambulance?” the instructor asked, but my dad vehemently refused.

“No, no. I don’t want to spend all that money. It’s just my back.”

The instructor looked hesitant. “Are you sure?”

My dad nodded and stuck his hand out for a handshake. He winced again when the instructor shook his hand. My dad turned to me and said, “Alright, let’s get out of here.” My dad heavily leaned on me as we practically crawled back to the car. I helped him into the driver's seat, and he looked pale as he struggled to put on his seatbelt.

"Can you even drive, Dad?"

He nodded and mumbled under his breath, "Why did I let him talk me into this?"

My dad barely talked to me over the next few days. He was laid up in his bed with his computer on his lap. The only time I talked to him was when he asked me to bring up a new ice pack. I'd ask him how he was feeling, and he'd mumble something along the lines of "Same old, same old." Meanwhile, throughout those long days, I'd lounge on the couch, considering even the weather was gloomy, too. I'd endlessly scroll through the channels and find something to watch, just waiting for my dad to call me back upstairs again. Just when I got a glimmer of hope from him, it was taken away.

After a week, he was finally getting better and not confined to his bed. Though that didn't change his routine much, seeing as he still locked himself away in his room, typing at his desk. A few more days went by and I couldn't take it anymore. The door to his room was shut, but I rushed in anyway. I grew tired of not knowing what he was writing, what was taking up so much of his time that he left me alone for hours on end when we were supposed to be doing things together.

"Are you ever going to let me read your stories?" I asked.

He closed his laptop and spun around, as if what he was writing was top secret. "I'm just not ready to share them yet. I need to perfect them a little more." Based on that response I doubted I'd ever read them, and I knew I didn't care enough to ask him again.

Seconds away from walking away, a flash of anger coursed through me. "I didn't come all the way here to be bored out of my mind all summer while you sit and type away all day. You barely spend any time with me, and when you do, it's like you'd rather do anything else. Do you even want me here?"

He raised his eyebrows and said, "I do. I'm sorry you've felt that way, that was never my intention. I love having you here, but I just don't know what you're interested in."

"Well, all you gotta do is ask."

"Okay, what are you interested in? What do you like to do?"

I thought about it for a moment, thinking of what we could realistically do in this small town. "I like soccer. I heard there was a game in a few hours."

"Do you want to go?" he asked, as he stood up from his chair.

"I do."

"Well, let's go then."

The bleachers were unbearably hot as we sat down in the back. Before the game even started, I had sweat pouring down my face. My dad had sweat beads pooling on his forehead as he watched the players line up on the field, just a few minutes away from starting.

"Did you ever play soccer, Dad?"

My dad nodded, the crinkles by his eyes exaggerated by the bright sun. "Played in college."

My eyes went wide. "Seriously? I didn't know that."

"Yep, played offense. That's actually how I met your mom."

"Really?"

He nodded, and looked out at the field as he said, "I saw her in the stands, and I somehow was able to catch up with her afterward. She came to every game I had from then on." He smiled fondly before directing his attention back towards the game, dropping the conversation.

The home team ended up losing, and while we were walking back to the car, my dad sure had a lot to say about it. More specifically, how our team could've performed better and how our defense was terrible.

After that day, we had some moments here and there. Near the end of summer, I convinced my dad to go to that comic bookstore, though he didn't care for it. While I wish I could say that the summer was memorable, it wasn't, and soon enough I was heading home with my mom. More than anything, I wanted to actually have a fun summer with my dad, but after the soccer game he reverted back to his usual self, leaving me to find ways to occupy my day.

The next summer, I didn't go stay with my dad. A few weeks before school ended, he called me and told me that he was going on a book tour. After years of rejections, he finally got published, and his agent was able to book him a tour to market his book. Originally, I was going to ask my dad if I could stay with Mom for the summer, so I was relieved that he told me this.

I loved being home that summer, hanging out with my friends, and not being bored for months on end. My dad called occasionally, although the calls were short. He sent me a copy of the book, though it ended up at the back of my bookshelf a few days later. At first, I wanted to read it, but then I thought about how he would choose to isolate himself in his room instead of being around his son. I hated that he wasted our summers, so I decided to wait to read it until I wasn't as mad anymore about the whole situation.

From then on, I never spent another summer with my dad. With that book being a success, he kept publishing more and more, and was busier than ever. Although we were never really close, this further separated us; his calls were less frequent, and he'd really only talk about work.

Every now and then, he'd come into town, and we'd watch a game together, though we never really were around each other for more than a couple of hours at a time sporadically throughout the year. Of course, he'd bring his new book, though I never got around to reading any of them.

When he died, I didn't know what I felt, which I know sounds awful. For some reason, he left me the house in Maine, so I headed up there to clean it out. The drive felt a lot longer now that I was the one driving, but soon enough I was back at the house.

He was a minimalist, so he didn't have many decorations. I walked around, trying to decide what room to tackle first. I decided to start with his bedroom and noticed a drawer of his desk was cracked open. I was about to close it when I saw a large stack of papers inside. I opened it further and grabbed the stack and put it on the desk. I pulled out the chair and sat down, flipping to the first page. It looked to be an unpublished book of his, and was frankly much different than what I expected. I'm not really sure what I thought he would write about, but within the first few pages, I realized this book was about me. The character's name was one of my old nicknames that he gave me when I was five. From skimming the first few pages, it seemed like he was retelling our arcade story with a few added details, and it made me wonder if he put any of our other memories in his stories.

He had all of his books on the bookshelf next to the desk, so I grabbed a couple, and I realized that each character was named from nicknames that he gave me as a child, and all of the books somehow had a memory of ours within them. I sat wide-eyed after reading each one. I had no idea that he cared this much, let alone enough to write stories about me.

Now, my dad wasn't an affectionate man, not even in the slightest, but I never knew that he could write something like this, or that he remembered all those memories. Flipping through these pages makes me wish that I would've read them sooner. These books were his way of trying to reach me, but I couldn't help but wish he made more memories with me while I was here. I flipped open his laptop, thankful I somehow knew the password, and saw several new stories waiting to be finished. I can't change our relationship now, but I could change the fact that some of these stories were waiting to be completed.

I cracked open the window, and the cool, salty breeze of the ocean brushed over me as I popped my knuckles and began typing. Tears welled up in my eyes as I now knew how he felt, and that I'll always have these stories with me even though he's not anymore, and now I can continue what he started.

I used to hate this house. When I first stepped inside, I was dead set on selling it, not wanting to spend another second here. But now? The for-sale sign has been yanked out of the earth and tossed in the trash. I can see why my dad lived in the silent house by the sea.

CHAPTER 8
Allergic

I found out who my new neighbors were when my son killed theirs. It was an accident, of course. My son gave theirs a peanut butter blossom cookie at recess, not knowing a bite of it would send him into shock. His parents, overwhelmed with moving into a new house the weekend before school started, forgot to pack his EpiPen in his backpack and his extra in his pants pocket. Their son died on the way to the hospital, and I didn't know about my son's involvement until twenty minutes before we left to head to the neighbor's house.

My son, Liam, had his suit on and was lying on his bed, crying his eyes out. He has always been a calm-mannered child, rarely throwing temper tantrums, but today he was inconsolable. I sat down next to him, wiping the tears off his red face, and asked if he didn't want to go. He didn't respond for a few minutes, and I figured the reason for his being upset was losing his friend. While he had only known Tatum for a day and a half, they had a lot of the same interests.

I poked his shoulder to get him to respond. "Can you tell me what's wrong, honey? Do you not want to go? We can stay home, Liam."

He shook his head. "It's not that, Mom. I think we should go."

"Okay, we can, buddy." I stood up, hanging by his doorframe before I said, "Let's head out in five minutes."

He nodded, and I was halfway down the hallway before he said in a broken voice that I've never heard from him before, "Mom, I think I killed him."

My stomach dropped at this, and I ran to his room, nearly running into the wall in the process. "What do you mean, Liam?"

He sat up, a new batch of tears running down his face, before he replied, "I gave him one of my peanut butter blossom cookies, Mom."

My heart sank. "Was he allergic?"

He shrugged his shoulders. "I don't know, but after he ate a bite, he started shaking."

"Were you in the classroom or outside at recess?"

"Recess."

My heart started pounding a little less. *Maybe it was a bee? A wasp? Something other than a peanut butter cookie that I made?* I swallowed a lump in my throat. "Are you sure it was the cookies, Liam? Maybe it was a bee?" I asked, trying to convince myself that it was the latter. He shrugged again. "Well," I said, "if it was the cookie, you didn't mean to, okay? You didn't know."

He attempted a smile and wiped his damp face once more. He stood up and wrapped his arms around me as tight as he could, almost knocking the breath out of me.

I said, "It's okay, honey. Let's not tell the Johnsons, okay? No reason to make them more upset than they already are, alright?"

"Okay, I won't, Mom."

I breathed out a sigh of relief. I glanced down at my shaking hands, quickly realizing they were going to be a problem if I didn't get a grip on myself. There was no reason to freak out yet; maybe it wasn't Liam's fault.

Liam and I were on their front porch a few minutes later. Awkwardly ringing the doorbell, waiting to meet new, heartbroken neighbors under such terrible circumstances. I hated that I was coming into their house harboring this. The door swung open a couple of seconds later, confused looks on their faces at the sight of two strangers. Tears welled up in the mother's eyes before the father asked, "I'm sorry, who are you?"

My cheeks flushed with embarrassment, momentarily wishing I never stepped foot on the porch. But if I didn't, my son wouldn't get closure.

"I'm sorry to bombard you like this, but my son, Liam, was actually in the same class as your son and was starting to become friends with him. We just wanted to pay our respects, but we totally understand if you don't want us here."

The mom sniffled; a small smile reached her face for a brief moment. "Why wouldn't we want you here? If you were Tatum's friend, even for a short while, you are welcome here."

The Johnsons let us inside. My mind was frazzled at her comment; my mind immediately turned to her figuring out my son's potential involvement in her young son's death, but there was no way of her knowing that. I brushed it off and Liam took off to mingle with the other kids while I glued myself to Mrs. Johnson. I sat down next to her on the couch, directly in front of all their family photos that included their three children. It appeared that Tatum was the oldest and had two toddler siblings.

"With the move and corralling my three kids, I almost didn't enroll Tatum in school." Mrs. Johnson breathed out, her voice shaky as she tried to get out each word. "Pre-K was a nightmare for me. Tatum kept getting exposed and I was terrified of sending him to school every day. But he loved all of it. From making friends to interacting with his teacher, he would be in school all day if we'd let him."

I wanted to console Mrs. Johnson but feared she wouldn't take too kindly to a stranger-turned-neighbor holding her hand soothingly only minutes after meeting. Instead, I listened to her intently, knowing that she had kept this inside over the past few days and didn't know who to talk about this with. Guilt spread inside me like wildfire as I waited to hear the rest of her monologue.

She said, "He was hospitalized a few times during Pre-K and kindergarten, each instance worse than the last. I brought up homeschooling to Tatum so that we could monitor his exposure, but he cried and cried. He wanted to make new friends since we moved away from all of his old ones." She paused for a second and tried to recompose herself. "I should've been more adamant about it. This wouldn't have happened had he been at home with me. Or if I remembered to pack his EpiPens. But it was a new backpack, and I was so concerned about getting him out the door that the thought never crossed my mind. I was just hoping that the other parents would've closely read the allergy list before packing their kids' lunches. It's not asking for much to not pack certain things in a lunchbox."

She sighed, running a trembling hand across her face.

I couldn't help myself for asking, but I needed to get to the bottom of the "exposure" she was mentioning. "I'm sorry, but what was Tatum allergic to?"

She looked more upset at that moment, but replied quickly, “Peanut butter.”

I nodded, but the breath in my lungs evaporated suddenly. It was Liam’s fault; even though he had no intention of hurting Tatum. We sat in an awkward silence for a bit. *Should I tell her?*

Before I could continue my spiraling, she said, “I just wish I could know who brought the cookies, which parent was irresponsible enough to cause my son to lose his life.”

She started crying once more, and before I had the chance to stop myself, I blurted out, “It was Liam who brought the peanut butter cookies. I made them, but we didn’t know he was allergic. I’m so sorry.”

I said it in one breath, hoping my honesty would be my saving grace.

Her husband reached me in a few strides, his hand on my back in a gentle but firm way as he led me to the door. I felt my cheeks burn with embarrassment and shame as all eyes turned on me. “I’m sorry, I didn’t mean to. Please, I--”

“I don’t give a shit about your apologies, get the fuck out of my house,” Mrs. Johnson shouted. “And get your son out of here, too. Stay the fuck away from my family. You’ve caused enough damage.”

Soon enough, I was staring at their front door as it slammed shut on me and Liam. He looked up with glassy eyes before mine soon filled with tears.

God, what have I done?

CHAPTER 9

The Door

For as long as I remember, I was scared of this door. There was nothing different about it. It looked like every other normal door. But I distinctly remember the first time I was scared of it.

I think my fear of the door spurred from my mother forcefully telling me not to open it, even if it was just a crack. Anytime I'd walk too close she'd grab me by the arm, hard, speaking through her teeth to get away from it, to ignore any sounds I might hear on the inside.

My mom worked overtime most days and I had a babysitter practically ninety-percent of my childhood. My babysitter, Vicky, would try to distract me from my mother's absence by playing a game each night. Any time Vicky came over, she'd remind me to stay away from the door, obviously following my mother's instructions.

We lived in a small one-bedroom house, so we never had room to play hide and seek. But she was more creative than that. I never knew if she genuinely wanted to be babysitting on her school nights, but she always came over with a smile on her face.

That night we spiced it up with a new game. That game was creating paper airplanes and seeing whose could fly the farthest. Nothing too exciting, but enough to keep me entertained for a couple of hours. We played that for a while, and then took a break when she made me what she called her famous mac 'n' cheese (it was actually Kraft). After about an hour of playing, we decided to create an obstacle course for the planes, which was really throwing the planes through a bent hula hoop.

"No!" Vicky yelled. I was holding the hula hoop above my head, and she had thrown her plane and it looked like it was going through the hoop before it dove down suddenly. She grabbed her plane, fixed the bent tip and was about to throw it again before she stopped and said, "Jesse, why don't you throw now? You've been holding the hoop for the past ten minutes."

I liked holding the hoop because I had a feeling that her paper airplane was better than mine. My first few throws weren't all that great, and seeing now that we had to throw it through a hula hoop, I doubted my plane's ability even more.

I stood behind our makeshift sock line starting point and, without even practicing, I threw the plane. It was a wobbly throw, but to my surprise it somehow went through the hoop and the full length of the hallway.

Vicky cheered and clapped for me as I went to retrieve my plane. I grabbed it carefully, not wanting to crumple it in any way, when a shiver rushed down my spine. Goosebumps covered my neck as I looked up to see the blue door in front of me. My mom told me the room was off limits when we moved in, and it was always locked. I was fine staying away, but my mind would drift about what was on the other side of the door. Could it be my mom's junk closet, so she'd tell me not to go in to avoid hurting myself? I'd often tell myself that's what it was, to shove down my curiosity, to try to ignore it as much as I could.

For tonight, I decided to give myself some distance from the door, so I told Vicky I wanted to stop playing. She nodded, her hands on her hips, before a smirk appeared on her face.

"Oh, I see, you're wanting to leave it on a high note? Make sure I don't beat you, is that it?"

I agreed, even though it wasn't the truth and thankfully she dropped the conversation. I told her I wanted to be in the living room for the rest of the night, which sparked a puzzled look on her face, considering I always liked to be running around. But she simply said, "Sure thing, kiddo. How about you pick out a movie?"

I nodded, needing a distraction. I plopped down on the floor and perused our long collection of DVDs and picked a few at random. Our movie nights were rare, but when we did, I would choose a few movies and we'd narrow down which one we wanted.

For tonight, I was debating between The Lion King, Pirates of the Caribbean, and Ratatouille. I set them in front of her and we gave each other a look, knowing the clear choice was Pirates of the Caribbean. I popped in the movie while she made a heaping bowl of popcorn, and we settled on the couch. We watched the film for a few minutes before she pulled out her backpack. I turned to her, already fully aware that she was pulling my backpack out for me, too. I groaned, and she shook her head before saying, "Hey now, I have homework too, so you won't be alone. I promised your mom that you'd get it done before she came back."

I ripped the backpack from her hands and hurriedly finished it. She gave me a look when I shoved my homework back in my backpack less than fifteen minutes later, but let it go as I became absorbed into the movie. Two hours flew by, and my mom was late as usual. Once 10 p.m. rolled around my mom would let Vicky go home for the night, leaving me by myself until she got back. I hated when Vicky left; I never knew when my mom would come back, so most nights I'd stay awake until I heard her unlock the door.

"Come on, Jesse. I have to get home." Annoyance rang in her voice as I kept her car keys away from her. With the eerie feeling from the hallway door, the last thing I wanted was to be by myself. I held onto her keys, and she tried to snatch them out of my hands and partially succeeded when I accidentally threw them across the hallway.

"Gosh, Jesse. Can you grab those for me?"

I turned back and saw that they landed in front of the door. I shook my head, and her eyebrows raised. She sighed and grabbed the keys herself. She stopped for a second as she bent down to grab them before she stood up and walked back towards me.

"Alright, well, I gotta get going now. Will you be alright being by yourself?"

I nodded reluctantly and she waited for me to lock the front door to leave. I laid against the door, my heart rate rising as I stood alone. I looked over at the clock in the kitchen and it read 10:05 p.m. I sighed, knowing that if my mom wasn't back by now, she wouldn't be back for several more hours. My eyes were glued to the blue door as I made my way to the room we shared. I had a bed pressed up against the wall and my mom's was on the opposite side.

I never understood why we shared a room, especially when I had a feeling that the room beyond the door wasn't just a storage room. I craved my own space, and wondered if this room could provide it. I laid down in my bed, my covers pulled tight on top of me like they would protect me. I tried to close my eyes, but I couldn't shake off the feeling that I needed to investigate. I huffed and threw my blankets off and peeked my head around the bedroom doorframe. With Vicky gone, I could get a little closer, put my ear against the door.

That would be fine. I'm just listening. I'm not opening it.

Goosebumps riddled my skin once more and I fought against every bone in my body, telling me to stay put. *It couldn't be bad, it's just a room.* If I could see what was inside, I wouldn't think twice about it again.

I took a few more steps towards the door, taking one step too close, and I ended up kicking it. I gasped as it popped open an inch.

I tried to look in, but the dimming hallway light didn't provide me with enough light to see what was inside. Instead, I put my ear against the door and heard slight wheezing.

I covered my mouth, thinking it could've been my erratic breathing, but after I waited for a few seconds, the slow and steady wheezing continued.

CHAPTER 10
Whispers

When I was younger, I lived outside. My feet were always bright green with grass stuck in between my toes, and I always had sweat dripping down my sunburned cheeks. I did everything I could outside, whether that was playing on the swing set, kickball, or chasing my dog around the yard. I made sure I was outside from sunrise to sunset. But my favorite thing was being in the garden.

I loved playing with the bugs and watching the flowers grow. My mom had a beautiful garden that she maintained every year, and each year it would grow bigger and bigger. Once I started taking an interest in it, she'd let me pick a new plant and we'd watch its progress. We'd maintain a few plants, and each morning my mom and I would race outside to see our little plants growing.

This continued well throughout my childhood and into my teens, and when it came time to attend college, it was a no-brainer what I was going to study: agriculture. Specifically, I wanted to be an agronomist where I could conduct crop experiments, solve problems related to harvesting, planting... well, practically anything to get me in a lab.

I was ecstatic when I had my first day in the lab. While the lab coat and oversized goggles were less than glamorous, I was in heaven. For the first couple of years, I had the lab to myself. I loved it; just me and the plants were all I needed. My hard work didn't go unnoticed, and after applying and winning a multi-million dollar grant to further fund my research, my boss decided to hire a protégé for me to manage. Well, he wasn't really a protégé, just a graduate student, but I didn't realize how much I actually liked working alone until his chipper attitude burst into the lab.

After a week, I told my mom about how much Andrew, the graduate student, annoyed me.

"Oh, don't be so harsh, Amelia," my mom said, as she started setting the dinner table. I always joined my mother for dinner on Wednesdays, and like usual, she made her famous spaghetti. "He's only been there a month, right? He's probably still adjusting to things."

"I know, but if you could be there for a few minutes you'd understand. It was much better when I worked by myself."

"It does you good to have Andrew in there. You shouldn't be alone all the time, honey." She put some spaghetti on both of our plates, a devilish smile growing on her face, before she asked, "Is he cute?"

I rolled my eyes and muttered, "Mom, he works for me."

"So?"

I sighed, knowing she wasn't going to easily let up. "Can we just talk about something else?"

"Oh, fine. Tell me about some of the things you've been doing in the lab."

I started explaining my work over the past few weeks and she simply nodded along, not understanding in the slightest, but listening regardless. I left a little over an hour later and returned to my own garden back at my house, filled up the watering can, and took it outside. Luckily, it was still light out, and I was able to admire my blooming blueberry plant.

Out of all my plants, my blueberry plant was my favorite. I remember the first year I ever tried to grow a garden. I decided to go small and not take on as much so I wouldn't get too overwhelmed, and I went with a single blueberry plant. I stayed by that plant all summer long and I guarded it from the animals trying to eat it, from bugs, from bad weather, you name it. While it only yielded eighteen blueberries, I was still proud, nonetheless. Excitement flooded through me every time a new blueberry sprouted. From then on, my blueberry plant grew more and more, and soon enough I had well over two hundred.

That's the plant I heard the voice from first.

That evening, I was staring at the plant fondly when I heard a little voice whisper, "Hey."

I gasped and whipped my head around, thinking it must've been one of the neighborhood kids sneaking up on me. From time to time, they liked to pull pranks on me, so I figured they somehow opened my gate and waltzed into my backyard. I got up to investigate, my heart beating wildly as I saw the gate was closed. I shook my head, tried to calm myself down, and plopped down by my blueberry plant again.

I almost finished watering all the plants when I heard another tiny whisper, "Hey, Amelia!"

I jumped back and scanned around, hoping to actually see someone around me. Again, nobody was there, so I slapped my face lightly in an effort to wake myself up. Perhaps I was nodding off and was dreaming of hearing those things? *I've been pulling a lot of late nights at the lab, and clearly it has caught up with me.*

I decided to go to bed early that night and woke up the next morning refreshed, feeling like a new person. I guess it was obvious how sluggish I had been because Andrew even picked up on it by saying, "You seem more chipper than normal."

"Finally caught up on sleep."

He nodded. "Good, you've been overworking yourself."

By catching up on sleep I was able to get a lot more work done than I had in weeks. Over a few hours, I finally finished writing a proposal for research funding that I meant to complete over two weeks before. I explained that after Andrew stepped foot in the lab, we had made significant progress. I'll admit, while he could be annoying to get along with, he is a hard worker and because of all his work, we had completely blown through the money. Our lab focused on finding ways to sustainably grow plants to increase their output without any nasty chemicals. So, now we needed more money fast, or else we would have to stall our research.

After submitting the proposal, I redirected my focus back onto one of the crops I was experimenting on, when I heard a tiny voice whisper, "Amelia."

I widened my eyes and glanced over at Andrew, who was not paying attention to me in the slightest, and asked him, "Did you say something?"

Andrew glanced over at me and took out the headphones that I didn't even know he was wearing, and he said, "I'm sorry, what?"

I repeated my question, and he shook his head. "Nope, not me."

I clicked my tongue and took a step back from the lab before instructing Andrew to finish my experiment for the day. I decided to go to my mom's house for a surprise visit. While she could get on my nerves sometimes with her million questions, she calmed me down more than anything.

I knocked on the door and she opened it, confusion written on her face, considering I was at her door in the middle of the afternoon. This was very unlike me.

"Are you going to let me in?" I chuckled. My mom shook her head and waved me in before closing the door.

"Sorry, honey. You've just never come by during the day." She began walking down the hall before abruptly stopping and turning around. She grabbed my shoulders and said, "Is everything okay?"

I knew this would freak her out, so I tried to reassure her the best I could. "Yes, Mom, I promise. I decided to take a half day and give myself a break for once."

A smile flashed on her face upon hearing this. She finally let go of my shoulders and took a step back, emitting a relieved sigh as she turned back around and led us to her kitchen. She stood behind her counter while I pulled out a stool and sat down.

"You had me worried there, I'm glad to hear everything's okay. So, why did you decide to take some time off?"

"I've been overworking myself and I think it's finally caught up to me."

"You deserve some time off, how much are you taking?"

"Well, I have a lot of PTO saved up, so I was thinking of taking a week or two for a real vacation. Maybe I could go somewhere warm, like Florida, and relax on the beach for a while."

Her eyes widened at this, and I could tell she was refraining from asking me if she could tag along, but I didn't want to go by myself, so I asked her if she wanted to join, too. She squealed in excitement.

"Oh, I'm so excited, I can't wait to contact my travel agent and get this process started!"

"No, don't worry about it, I'll make sure everything is booked. Just worry about packing," I said.

"I can do that, thank you for inviting me to come, sweetie. We will have such a great time." She smiled before rounding around the counter to hug me.

My mom has always been the type of person who needs to keep busy, especially when she was excited, to blow off some steam, so she grabbed a few of her tomatoes to cut them. My heart dropped when she pulled them out of the fridge, as it reminded me of the last two weird interactions I've had with plants. While I was excited about the trip, and clearly my mom was, too, the thought of those whispers lingered in the back of my mind. So, I decided to rip off the Band-Aid and ask if she's had any weird experiences.

"Mom..." I hesitated, unsure of how she would respond to such an offbeat question.

"Yes, what is it, dear?" she replied sweetly, as she was washing some of her freshly grown tomatoes.

"Have you ever talked to your plants?"

She turned the water off and set her tomatoes on a cutting board.

"Talked to my plants? Can't say that I have. Why, do you?" She giggled at this.

I shook my head and replied, "No, one of my coworkers does all the time. Claims that it talks back."

"Hmm, weird. Maybe you should try to get out there and out of that lab more."

I figured she would try to slide in one of her usual comments of how I need to get myself out there and meet someone. Seeing as I'm approaching thirty years old and no marriage in sight, she's been peppering in these suggestions and questions not-so-subtly in nearly every conversation we have, just like she had a few weeks prior. But at least this one was fairly harmless, especially since she followed it up with:

"At least now you can, with our trip!"

Within the week we were sitting on the beach, the sun beating down on our skin, certain to give us some horrific sunburns. My mom sat beside me, reading one of the many books that she brought on the trip, while I simply basked in the sun. I didn't realize how much I needed the break until I sat down on that beach chair, without a care in the world.

We continued this routine for a few days until we got tired of laying on the beach for hours. Our sunburnt skin would surely be thanking us for a bit of a break from the hot sun as we decided to tour around Largo, Florida, and see what the city had to offer.

I truly didn't care what we did, so I had my mom decide. I knew that whatever I decided she'd find a problem with, so it was easier to just let her pick, as I knew she would want to do something new every day. One day we visited a museum, while the next we went to a boardwalk that had a bunch of shops, and then another day, it rained, so we cozied up in the hotel room. But letting her choose our daily activities proved to be a mistake on one of the last days of our trip, as she suggested going to the botanical gardens. I was very hesitant about going and told her she could go without me if she wanted, but she protested.

"Oh, you have to go, Amelia! It's one of the best botanical gardens in Florida. You can't miss out!"

"There are other botanical gardens that I could visit, Mom." I rolled my eyes as she sat on my bed with pleading eyes. She had an ornery look on her face, and I knew she wasn't going to let up, so after probably a half an hour debate, I finally gave in.

My mom clapped with excitement and rushed to get ready while I remained on the bed, anxious about how the day was going to play out.

I tried to set my nervousness aside and take in the 182 acres of the gardens. My mom was over the moon; I don't think I had seen her that happy in a long time. Thankfully, there were not a lot of people there since it was a blistering day out, but that only meant we got to see the flowers with ease. My mom could've stared at dahlias, her favorite flower, for hours, and broke away from me to gaze at them. I got a little overheated and sat down by a bed of some flowers to cool down. I leaned on the burning pavement, feeling the sweat drip down my forehead, as I watched my mom seemingly unfazed by the heat. Of course, she had brought a little portable fan with her, so she stood happily by the flowers.

I closed my eyes for a second and began to zone out, until I heard my name screamed loudly. I flung my eyes open and looked around, and saw my mom was in the same position she was in earlier. I narrowed my eyes and called out, "Did you say something?"

She turned her head in my direction and walked over towards me. "What did you say?"

"I asked if you said something."

She shook her head. "No, I didn't." She looked at my face for a couple of seconds before saying, "Why don't you take my little fan? You're a bit sweaty, sweetheart. I don't want you to overheat." She handed me the fan, and I'll admit, I did feel a little better. "Do you mind if I walk around for a bit while you cool off?" she asked.

"Yeah, that's fine. I'll stay here."

She left and I angled the fan to blow the cold air on my face. I closed my eyes, as the air was drying out my contacts, when I heard in a louder tone, "Amelia! Oh, Amelia!" I squeezed my eyes tighter, hoping I could block the sound. "Listen, Amelia. Why won't you listen?"

At this point, I stood up, dropping the fan as I scrambled to get away, but the voices roared louder. I dropped to my knees on the pavement, surely skinning them as I covered my ears, muffling their whispers of, "Amelia! Come closer!"

I felt a hand grasping my shoulder tightly and I lifted my head to see my mom's concerned face. "You okay, honey?"

I nodded and tried to slow my breathing and calm myself down. She grabbed the fan off the ground and angled it towards my face once more. She took her hand off my shoulder and reached for my hand before she said, "Why don't you just come sit down on this ledge."

I shook my head at this, and she added, "Honey, you're awfully pale. I'm afraid you have heatstroke or something. Come and sit down." She pulled my hand and dragged me towards the ledge and sat me down. I tried to focus on her voice, but the voices of the plants only intensified. After a minute went by, I couldn't handle it. I felt like I couldn't escape from it, so I quickly got up and left. My mom called after me as I wove through the crowd to put some distance between myself and those plants.

Evidently, I collapsed after making it through the entrance. The ambulance was called, and I was diagnosed with a panic attack. A large hospital bill later and we made it back to our hotel room. My mom was watching over me intently the rest of the night before I asked, "What is it, Mom?"

"I've just never seen you like that, sweetie. You scared me."

"I know, I'm sorry."

She sat down at the edge of my bed.

"What happened?" she asked.

I didn't want to hit her with the truth, because it still didn't make any sense to me, so I instead said, "I think the heat just got to me. Not used to it being this hot."

She didn't look convinced, but she dropped it.

We left a few days later, and I took an extra few days off, needing some time to be by myself. I did enjoy the trip, but that encounter at the botanical gardens stressed me out because I didn't know what I would face back at the lab. The days that I took off were filled with anxiety, and for the first time in my life, I didn't tend to my garden. I stayed inside the house the entire time and peered at my dwindling plants from the window. I wanted so badly to take a watering can to them, but I was terrified of what I would hear. I hoped that if I gave myself a break from the plants, maybe those voices would subside.

It felt weird to have the wind on my face that next morning after being cooped up in the house. I looked up at the sky, curious if a storm was approaching, based on how windy it was. The sky was clear, but the wind blew my lanyard out of my hand and onto the grass. I bent down and scooped up my lanyard when I heard screams filling my ears. I fell back onto the grass, and the screams grew louder. I whipped my head around to see if anyone was around me and saw no one. The longer I sat on the grass, the screaming intensified, and it felt like my eardrums were about to burst. I scrambled up, covered my ears, and sprinted to my car.

I slammed the door and took a few heavy breaths of relief when the screaming died down. I drove to work, my nerves shot, as I was hoping for a calm morning but had quite the opposite.

I took a big swig out of my coffee as soon as I stepped foot in the lab, and Andrew raised his eyebrows.

"You look even more stressed than before the vacation. Did it go that bad?"

I made up the excuse that I caught food poisoning while we were there, and he cringed.

"Well, you do look pale. Are you feeling any better?"

"Yeah, still not the best though," I lied, as I set my bag down on the counter.

He nodded and quickly changed the conversation. "Do you mind if I walk through some things with you? Truthfully, I wasn't able to get a lot done without you here."

I internally rejoiced when he said this, because this was one of the things that had circled through my mind over the last few days. I knew I needed to teach Andrew more, and I guess I didn't want to admit it until then. Instead of being happy in the lab, I had come to dread it. And if it came to it, I might need to step away from the lab for longer than two weeks.

I tried not to be irrational, so I showed up and worked my usual hours for the next couple of weeks to teach Andrew. I could hear the whispers from the plants as clear as ever, despite trying to block them out. It was agonizing being in the lab. While I would attempt to teach Andrew, I continually became distracted because I couldn't block the voices out.

Instead of hearing the voices at random times, it was constant in the lab. And as soon as I'd get home, the grass would be screaming at me. It got to the point where the only time I'd get relief would be in my car. It used to be my house, but I had to throw my fake plants out, too.

I resorted to blasting music in my headphones for the majority of the day, but all that managed to do was cause tinnitus and annoy my boss any time he wanted to talk to me. I found myself taking more sick days, needing a relief from the whispers. I'd research plant-less areas and grappled with the idea of moving, to escape the only place I've known for an ounce of peace. Many sleepless nights later, I quit. Over the course of a few weeks, I transitioned Andrew enough to where he could take my job. I'm sure my boss thought I was having a mental breakdown when I announced that Andrew would now have my position, considering how hard I worked for it. It killed me that I had to leave, but my sanity was more important, and who knows? Maybe I can find a new passion.

I packed my bags into my car and into the U-Haul. My mom decided to move with me, to keep an eye on me. *But it should get better now,* I thought. *I'll fill my days with new hobbies, find a different career.*

The screaming from the grass subsided as I plugged in the address of my new home. I didn't want to move, but it was worth a shot.

I'll figure this out, I'll be more peaceful now.

I just need these voices gone. I just want them gone.

CHAPTER 11
Tyler

My parents sealed a little door off in my closet years ago. Behind all of my clothes, shoes, and miscellaneous stuff in my closet, there's a white, tiny door painted to blend in with the closet. I had lived in that house for five years before noticing, and I only noticed it when my mom made me go through my closet.

Normally, I had a bunch of clothes stacked on the floor. But after moving them to the side and ducking my head down to check for any last remaining clothes, something shiny reflected in the back of the closet. I scrunched my eyes and reached forward, unsure of what it was. Once I finally touched it, I realized it was a small doorknob. I tried to give it a push and twisted the knob, then I kicked the door hard enough for the paint to crack, the door to groan, and voila, the tiny door opened. Dust spewed everywhere. I was planning on keeping the room a secret, but after I inhaled all of that dust and went into a coughing fit, my mom ran upstairs to see what the problem was. She saw me crouched down in the closet, about to cough up a lung.

"What on earth is going on in here, Tommy?" she asked, then she bent down and saw that small door cracked open. Her eyes widened and she called for my dad.

He ran upstairs and muttered under his breath, "How the hell did we not notice this?"

"I'm not sure. Do you think it's safe?" my mom asked.

"It should be fine. Why don't you clean it up for him?"

I nodded enthusiastically at this, and my mom and I spent the rest of the afternoon cleaning up the little room. We probably knocked down over a hundred cobwebs and sneezed a dozen times before we finally got it all cleaned up. I put some of my books and games in there, determined to make it my own little hideaway from the rest of my family. I spent a lot of time in the room, and as soon as I would get home from school I would plop down in there.

After a month of enjoying the space, though, Tyler appeared.

I had a long week at school and was startled to see a boy, who looked around my age, sitting in the corner. I jumped back and he giggled, putting his hand on his mouth when he saw my surprise. I ducked down and stepped inside.

"Who are you?" I asked.

He smiled wide and said, "Tyler."

"What are you doing here?" I asked.

"To come play with you."

I nodded and went along with it. After the first appearance, he came every day. We'd spend hours in there, either playing games or watching TV. He was like a brother I never had. All I had was a little sister, Teagan, but since she just turned one, I couldn't really play with her yet. Our favorite game to play was Sorry. We'd play it several times when I'd get home from school. He loved it so much that he'd become upset when I had to go to bed. Big tears would fall down his face each night when my mom would tell me that it was time for bed. At first, he was fine with me leaving, but the longer he stayed in that room, the worse and lonelier he got.

One night, after probably seven rounds of Sorry, he wailed when my mom called for me. My eyes widened and I shushed him, as my parents didn't know about him.

"Tyler, come on, I'll be back tomorrow. Don't be upset."

"You always leave me, Tommy." He sniffled and wiped the back of his hand on his nose.

"I'm sorry, Tyler. I have to go to bed."

He cried harder at this and whispered, "You'll leave me like they did. I just know it."

Before I had time to respond, my mom burst into the room. "Tommy, I thought I told..." She yelled before stopping in her tracks. Her hand slapped on her mouth as she gasped.

"Tommy, get out of there."

I remained seated and my mom yelled, "Tommy, now!"

I crawled out and she slammed the door immediately. She bent down in front of me, her hands gripping my shoulders tightly as she shakily said, "Tommy, you are never to go in there again. Do you understand?"

I protested at this and responded, "I can't just leave Tyler in there, Mom. He can't be by himself."

My mom's face paled at this. "Tyler?" she choked out.

"Yeah, Tyler," I repeated.

"Listen, Tommy, I don't want you going in there, end of discussion," she said.

I gulped and nodded. But after a few days of his constant wails, his sputtering sobs that seemed more and more distraught, I cracked open the door. Tyler sat in a corner, tears down his translucent face before I brought a pillow and blanket inside and curled up beside him. He doesn't cry anymore, and I spend all my nights in that little closet, with the ghost of my brother, Tyler.

CHAPTER 12
Names

J*ade*

An eight-month relationship in high school is different than an eight-month relationship when you're 27. Don't think so? Let me explain why.

When I was in high school, I dated this girl for that amount of time, give or take. I wasn't committed; I kind of liked her most of the time. But I had options. Hell, I was only 17.

But then, when I was 27, I broke up with a girl because I thought I *still* had a lot of options. After months went by, and I realized I didn't, I crawled back to her. When she didn't take me back, I was terrified. Not only did I ruin my chance with her, but I couldn't find anyone to replace her.

Until that day.

I yanked open the door to my local coffee shop and stood in line. I scanned the menu, or at least pretended to. I wasn't a fan of coffee, but I couldn't just stay here for hours without buying anything. There was barely anyone in here: a few tired customers, two baristas, and of course, her, sitting in the back.

My order was a simple black coffee. If I was going to try to talk to her for a few hours, I had a feeling I would need something stronger than the mocha that I'm sure was in her cup. I could feel her eyes on me while I waited for the overpriced coffee. I'd glance back towards her here and there, show her I had some interest while not being too overbearing. She was attractive enough. Cared a lot about her appearance and did everything she could to get a few minutes of attention from guys. I was a few feet away from her, yet I could still tell she had fake eyelashes, dirty blonde hair with extensions, and clothes so tight they left nothing to the imagination. She tried to stand out, but that's what drew me to her. She was a try-hard, so I wanted to show her why that wouldn't work on me.

I grabbed my steaming cup and sat down in a booth a few away from her. Her attention was piqued, her eyes glancing above her laptop to see what I was doing. I sat around for a few minutes, casually sipping on my bland coffee while scrolling through my phone. Her eyes kept darting up, and after the fifteenth time in ten minutes, I got up and slid into her booth. Her pens and papers were scattered across the grimy table like she was trying to seem busier and more intelligent than she actually was.

Her eyes widened underneath the fake prescription glasses she had on. She slowly took them off, setting them on a stack of paper on the table before she said, "Can I help you?"

She was confident, blunt, and probably annoyed that a more attractive guy didn't sit down and that I did instead. She probably thought I was hogging up her booth when, in actuality, there were no other guys in here other than the male barista in the back. But he was paying more attention to his phone than the orders. He wasn't even looking in her direction while, I was. With how many times she looked in my direction, I knew it wasn't a coincidence that we kept locking eyes. She was playing hard to get, when we both knew that wasn't the case.

"Just saw you across the room and had to come over."

"And why is that?" She leaned back against her booth, dragging her drink along the table before taking a long swig of it with a smirk.

"So, what brings you here to this coffee shop, Jade?" Jade narrowed her eyes before I pointed to the label on the side of her drink. She got a pumpkin spice latte. Looks like I guessed wrong about the mocha, but just from that I could tell she was more basic than I originally thought she was.

"Work," she said simply, uninterested in divulging anything else. I nodded and just stared at her, hoping the prolonged awkward silence would spark her to give me something else to work with.

I could tell she was still debating whether or not to kick me out of her booth, but as I said before, she liked attention, so she asked, "Now, what brings you here, Sam?" She was proud of herself, playing the same trick I did on her. She crossed her arms across her chest, glancing down at her unlocked phone that buzzed more than several times since I sat down with her. She was the type of girl who would talk behind her friend's back. At least that's what her text messages implied. Gossiping to one friend to another, running the thin line of accidentally texting the wrong one. I suppose that gave her a rush because that's all she did on that cracked phone of hers, in between waiting for my long-anticipated answer.

"Trying to get some inspiration."

She perked up at that, her eyes lighting up as she focused her attention on me.

"What for?"

"Work." Two can play at this game. This frustrated her a little bit.

But not enough, as she probed. "And what do you do?" she asked.

I clicked my teeth, shaking my head.

"Gotta tell me what you do first, only fair."

She mocked me and shook her head with a smile.

"I'm a writer..." She trailed off as though I would judge her.

I feigned interest and widened my eyes. "No way, really?"

She scooted forward and tilted her head slightly, before saying, "I work over at Daily Journal, a few streets over."

"What a coincidence. I work over at Wiley and write some articles for them." I rolled my eyes internally. Did I really work there? Of course not. No, that's what she wanted to hear. All girls want is someone they can relate to; it makes them feel more at ease to trust a stranger. That's how you hook them in, and from the looks of it, it was starting to work on her.

Now I didn't even have to ask her any more small-talk questions. She wanted to lead the conversation. "I generally work as a freelancer, but right now I'm contracted at the Daily Journal for the next few months."

"Seems like you must be a damn good writer to be a freelancer," I responded. She had a slight blush spanning her cheeks with this comment, but I could tell she was willingly bringing heat to her cheeks to seem modest. In reality, she was more than likely a bragging bitch that likes to gloat about the small--and I mean *small*--accomplishments she's had in recent years. I know it sounds like I made a quick judgment about her, and hey, I could be wrong.

She laughed me off, waving her hand around as if she was letting her guard down to me.

"I'm sure you are as well." She winked.

Although she was forward, I was surprised when she invited me over to her apartment. She eagerly packed her things up, crumpling her papers in her small pink purse as she scooted out of the booth. She linked her small arm around mine as she directed us to her place.

Her apartment was about what I expected it to be: quaint but vibrant. Pictures all over the brightly-colored walls, a cluttered but neat mess with random decor on the shelves, along with a few meaningless awards that caught my eye. Okay, they didn't really, but I knew she would make a fuss out of it if I didn't at least bring it up. So, I pointed at the awards she presented so proudly on those tiny shelves and asked, "Where'd you get these from?"

"Oh, those?" She plopped down on the couch, drinking the last bit of her coffee as she sat with her legs crossed, a grin playing on her delicate face. She explained each one in excruciatingly long detail, the grin on her face widening as it took all that it was in me to not scoff at her narcissistic monologue. They were basically departmental awards, encouraging her to stay in her shitty position, and praising her for work that high school students could do. But it had worked for her this long, I guess. I kept eye contact with her, portraying interest while I was feeling anything but.

My fingers ran along the random assortment of books she had lined up while she glanced up at me, curiosity playing across her green eyes.

"So, why is today the first time I've seen you at that coffee shop?" she asked, wrapping her arms around a pillow that was lying on her chest, her eyes motioning for me to join her instead of across the room like I had been. I sat down carefully, the fading brown couch clearly not big enough for the both of us--as my legs and ass half hung off--while she sat with her legs crossed underneath her, much more comfortable than I was.

"I was sick of sitting at my desk back at the office, I guess," I said. "It's an old stuffy building, with no scenery whatsoever. So, I thought, what better place to change things up than a coffee shop to people-watch? Maybe gain some inspiration, rather than staring at a white wall for eight hours a day."

She sat up, giving me more room as she moved her legs to the side. "That's why I go there, too. I used to work here at home, and I couldn't get anything done and be productive. I'd just lay in bed and fall asleep." She laughed, leaning her head on her hand that was resting on the couch.

I said, "I could tell you liked that coffee shop. I've seen you there for the past few weeks."

She narrowed her eyes and scooted farther back onto the couch, like it was supposed to give herself some distance. But, in reality, all it did was signify that she was closing herself off from me. I sighed internally. *Dammit, I might have blown it.* I quickly backtracked, seeing the gears in her brain close off more the longer I remained silent. I sucked in a breath, and let my pride loose by telling her that I'd walked past it a few times. She was often the only person in there, and clearly the most beautiful in the room, so I noticed her. She often sat in the same spot. After that embarrassing cover-up, she still looked nervous. So, I continued on, babbling that I was nervous around her, and spoke before I should, and that's she beautiful. *I can't really go wrong with complimenting her twice.*

Here's a quick tip: don't raise suspicion like I did. Try to reassure the best you can, but sometimes, you'll just have to cut your losses like I was about to. Luckily, she bought it and perked up again once I complimented her and called her beautiful. Twice. Which wasn't a lie at all, but I wasn't expecting her to forget what I said not even a minute before and throw caution to the wind and kiss me.

But there you go, that's how you fix it. Compliment her.

She pulled away a few minutes later, both of us a little too out of breath as a wide smile grew on her face.

I stayed for a while, a lot longer than I was expecting or hoping. She kept talking about herself, like I thought she would. After what must've been only twenty minutes--but felt like hours--she seemed at a loss for what else to brag about. Her personal life wasn't exciting, so I could see why she chose to sit in the coffee shop for hours on end. And if you wanted to know, I wasn't wrong. She went on and on about her career "accomplishments," but those really only consisted of certificate templates on Word, made by her coworkers, and the trophies were store-bought and still had the tags on them.

She's got some confidence, though; I'll at least give her that.

Allie

Not every girl is the same. I've learned that the hard way. You have to take a different approach, see what matters to them quickly, and harp on those to build a connection with them.

So, that's what I'm doing again now. Normally this would bother me, her being all over the place. Dropping shit left and right, silently apologizing to no one, while contemplating stepping around all the food she just dropped. But to me, it didn't matter that her brown hair was all matted up in her loose braid, or that her clothes were all baggy and did not at all conform to her body. She seemed more humble. Well, at least more than Jade.

We met in the canned food aisle. Romantic, I know. She had grabbed I-don't-know-how-many cans of green beans, corn, and beans, all stacked in her overfilling cart. She sighed, mumbling under her breath, shakily bending down to grab them as she tried to not let tears overflow.

I reached down before she did, brushing her hand as she gasped. She pushed her sunglasses up into her hair, pulling her zip-up hoodie closer to her frame. I set the cans in the cart, and a slight blush formed on her cheeks as she meekly smiled.

"Uh, thanks."

"Don't mention it." I smiled back. *You have to be subtle, don't want to come on too strong and scare her away.* She was more guarded and hesitant. I could tell from the rigidness of her shoulders and her shallow breathing that I made her nervous. So, I took a few steps back and told her to have a good rest of her day, giving her the space she needed. She nodded at this, wishing me the same as she slowly pushed the shopping cart to the checkout counter. A sigh emitted from her lips as she took in the total, most likely having to spend more than what she budgeted for.

I know what you're thinking. I could've stepped in and helped pay for some. I probably should've, but it would've been creepier if I did that, compared to what I did in the parking lot.

She struggled to push her cart back to her beat-up car, lifting up packages of water bottles and what appeared to be formula. I stood back. My car was a few down from hers, giving me the ability to look at her without her noticing me. She banged her hand on the trunk after dropping the cans again that she dropped earlier in the store. They rolled under the car slightly, just out of her reach, before I jogged over.

"Oh, you don't have to do that," she protested. But I was already on my knees, reaching under her small car to grab them. I gently set the cans in the car, staring up at her before I got back onto my feet. She tore her eyes away from mine, tears welling up in hers again as she wiped them away.

"Something tells me you don't want these cans," I joked, hoping to lighten her spirit.

A small smile reached her face as she said, "I guess not." She shook her head, looking down at my sweatshirt that was caked with dirt from the pavement. She tried to wipe it off with her hand, dust settling around us as she tried to pat some of it away.

"You didn't have to do that," she repeated, whispering.

"I wanted to." I refrained from stepping away. I could feel her closing off with each second that we stood there.

"Are you okay, uh..."

"Allie."

"Are you okay, Allie?" I already liked her much more than Jade. She wasn't looking for attention, she despised it. But I knew I just had to keep giving her a reason to trust me.

"It's just..." she sighed, rubbing her forehead. "It's just my parents left me in charge of all of my younger siblings, and they're never around to help. I'm having to work three jobs to take care of them."

She kept rambling on, and after five minutes, I stopped listening. Not because I didn't care, but through her intermittent small sobs and heavy breathing, I couldn't really understand what she was saying. What I did understand was that she was reaching her breaking point, and I wasn't sure if she would be able to stop.

A few minutes later, she stopped abruptly and widened her eyes. "I'm so sorry, I don't know why I unloaded all of that on you. I'm sure you have better places to be." She shifted the weight on her feet. "Thank you for all of your help," she added and closed the trunk of the car, but struggled slightly because of how crammed it was.

I grabbed her wrist, gently, and said, "I'm the oldest too. I raised my five younger siblings."

After I said that, it seemed like a huge weight was lifted off of her shoulders, and she could finally look me in the eye instead of the awkward eye contact she kept making with the ground. So, once again, I'll repeat this as much as I can: it's all about relating to them.

She walked over to the driver's side and stepped inside, shutting her car door. Her car took a few seconds to start and sputtered, while I glanced back and watched her sit and contemplate her next move. She was looking forward and rested her hands on her steering wheel. *Should be any second now, wait for it...*

"Wait!"

I grinned and slowly turned back, acting like I wasn't expecting that reaction. She threw open the car door, leaving her car running as I pretended to be shocked. "I know this is a little straightforward, but would you like to go to dinner with me sometime?" she asked breathlessly, putting a hand on her hip to regain some air in her lungs.

"I'd love to," I said.

She tore my phone out of my hands and plugged her number in, a smile on her face as she handed it back.

"Dinner at your place?" I winked. She took a few steps away, shaking her head bashfully as she yelled back.

"I'll text you!"

This one was gonna be a slow burner, unlike Jade. I'd have to take my time with Allie, and gain her trust over time, not in a matter of hours.

We had dinner a few days later at a local Italian restaurant. Before that, we texted nonstop. My fingers felt raw and a headache would appear any time I looked at a dimly-lit screen, but she seemed to never grow tired of it. She might take care of her siblings, but man, she sure found time to be on her phone.

The dinner went well, minus a few awkward silences, but mainly those came from her side, not mine. Being cooped up in the house all day or stuck at her jobs gave her nothing interesting to talk about, and she couldn't even really talk about herself. Any prying questions I would throw her way would easily be dodged and converted to something one of her siblings would say. After two hours of agonizing talk about everything but her, she finally opened up and realized not once had she talked about herself.

If you excuse the useless facts I found out about her little siblings, I found out that she was more quirky than I imagined. Loved older songs that went all the way back to the '70s, collected a bunch of old records, and, surprisingly enough, didn't want any kids. I'm not sure how we got on that topic; it was probably a rant after explaining her complicated and tiresome relationship with her younger siblings. But after she let loose and talked about herself, it was nearly impossible to get her to stop.

"I'm sorry. I'm doing it again, aren't I? Unloading way too much on you on a first date."

I grabbed her hand gently. "You're not unloading too much on me. I like hearing more about you."

She blushed at this and tore her hand away from mine. She set her hands in her lap in what I assume was an attempt to calm down or prevent me from feeling her clammy hands-- which I had already felt, by the way.

The rest of the night went fast, but our next date seemed to come by faster.

Aside from her talent for wrangling and battling kids all day, she was also somehow, good, at mini golf, which we decided to play the next night. Having not played a game in her life, each ball she made she would celebrate by jumping up and down as though she was a kid in a candy shop. Based on the weird and slightly judgmental stares we got, it seemed as if everyone else felt the situation was as odd as I did.

I guess I never took into consideration how much siblings can affect an older child's life, especially when you have to raise them by yourself. Being an only child, I never thought about it. Independence was something I always had, but for her, those moments seemed to be few and far between. So, instead of listening to the shitty, not-so-under-everybody's-breath comments, I soaked it in and enjoyed the small--but still over-the-top--celebrations that came with each hole.

We had just finished nine holes before we decided to sit down and take a break, debating if we should go on with the last nine. We got Dippin' Dots, something she had never had the pleasure of experiencing. I got cookies n' cream while she got chocolate chip cookie dough, and not too long after the cups were handed to us, they were gone. She smiled and shifted on the bench we had plopped down on, with some of her ice cream still on her face.

"As much as I love playing mini golf, I'm not sure if I wanna play another nine holes. The handle is starting to give me blisters," she said, looking down at her hands where some of the skin was already starting to redden.

"You read my mind," I replied. I grabbed her hand and she stood up, wrapping her arm around my torso as we found our way to the exit.

Our footsteps were quiet along the pavement, but my thoughts were loud in my mind with each step we took. She was so different than I thought she would be. Despite having to grow up early and take care of everyone, she still possessed that childlike wonder that most of us grow out of too quickly.

She leaned her head on my chest and snapped me out of my thoughts. She looked up with a smile on her face, while I returned one back. *She's being more affectionate and trustworthy than I thought she was going to be, not that I'm complaining.*

I thought it was going to take more than a few weeks, but I guess all it really does take is some amateur mini-golf and some melted Dippin' Dots.

Maren

Now the vulnerable ones, they're a different story entirely. They're more straightforward and to the point. But mainly, they just want some revenge. Or at least she did.

I wasn't planning this one, if I'm honest. But when you're seated in a restaurant, hearing the wails of a woman only a couple of tables away, you have to act. The woman, and what I assumed to be her boyfriend, had been fighting for the last thirty minutes before he left. And from the sounds of her boyfriend's--or maybe ex-boyfriend's?--yelling and abrupt exit, it sounded like they were hitting a rough spot. At first, she carried on eating her meal, as if she insisted that the food wouldn't be wasted. But in between her bites, tears were running down her face, so I doubt she was even enjoying it at all. Nobody else was helping her; the waiter seemed leery of her and only checked in every thirty minutes. But after the boyfriend left, he didn't come at all and just hung around the kitchen.

I debated going over. She was muttering to herself under her breath, shaking her head as she kept flinging her black hair over her shoulders to keep the long strands out of her food. It looked like spaghetti from a distance, but somehow it seemed even more unappetizing than my raw steak that had blood spewing out onto the plate with each bite.

I slowly slid into her booth, not wanting to scare or upset her any more than she already was. She looked up, a scowl on her face, before it softened.

“Sorry, I thought you were someone else,” she said.

“Boyfriend?” I asked.

She shook her head, a chuckle rising from her throat. “Ex-boyfriend. It seems like you were the only brave one to come over here.” She glanced around, a slight blush spanning her cheeks as she noticed several other couples looking at her. She tucked some hair behind her ear, trying to distract herself from everyone’s unrelenting stares.

I shook my head, trying to act modest. “I’m sure there were others, I was just close by.”

“You sure about that? My waiter looks like he’s been debating coming over for the last twenty minutes, too chicken to come over and console me. Guess we fought louder than I thought.”

“Probably just intimidated by your beauty,” I said. Cheesy, I know, but I figured she would like it.

She gave me a look, rolling her eyes with a slight grin before saying, “Smooth.”

“I try to be. So, what did your ex-boyfriend do?”

She narrowed her eyes and leaned forward on the table slightly, sliding her plate over to the side.

“Come on,” I added. “I know it wasn’t you that did anything.”

She teared up slightly before she said, “I don’t know why I’m crying over this. We’ve been broken up longer than we’ve been together.”

I refrained from grabbing her hand. “I’m sure it’s just a rough spot.”

She shook her head. “He cheated on me last week, and tried to make up for it by bringing me here.”

“Okay, I guess a major rough spot.” I said. She laughed, wiping underneath her eyes, missing some of the clumped mascara running down her cheeks. I scooted forward, carefully wiping away some black smudge from her bottom lashes. She leaned into my hand for a second before I scooted back. She gave me a small smile before she shakily raised her hand to move her hair out of her eyes, but it only fell back into place.

“It’s my fault really. I should’ve known. He was gone all the time, and never really wanted to be home. Talking about his coworker Lisa every chance he got.” she explained.

“It’s not your fault. Happens to the best of us.”

“Is that why you’re here alone?” She covered her mouth, seemingly punishing herself for saying that. “I’m sorry, I shouldn’t have asked you that.”

I waved my hand. “No, it’s fine. I’m actually in the same boat that you are. I booked this reservation a few months ago. It was supposed to be me and my girlfriend’s two-year anniversary, but she broke up with me last week.”

“I’m sorry to hear that.” She reached over and squeezed my hand lightly. I shrugged my shoulders. Truthfully, I hadn’t dated enough girls to be cheated on, unless they cheated on me and I didn’t know, which is entirely possible knowing my track record.

I ran my thumb over her hand. "Want to come over to my table? We don't want all of this food to go to waste, plus my waiter is a bit more friendly."

I winked and she giggled, contemplating for a second, before she untangled her hand from mine and reached over to grab her plate.

"No, no, I got it." I took the plate gently from her hands before adding, "Don't want you spilling that all over your beautiful dress."

She blushed at this and followed me the short distance over to my table. She slowly slid into the booth, sitting directly in front of me as she did earlier. She seemed more relaxed, as she wasn't under the scrutiny of the other people like she was before.

My waiter wasn't a coward like the last one. He came a few minutes after we got situated in the booth, refilling our waters as she took small bites of her meal. She set her fork down a few minutes later after an awkward silence, a slight grimace on her face.

I set down my fork as well, tired of chewing endlessly on the raw steak. "Not a fan of the food either?" I chuckled. Her face started to grow green with each bite, so I knew it was only a matter of time before she couldn't force it down anymore.

"You know, I've been talking to you for the past hour and never caught your name," she said, leaning her head on her hand as a small smirk rose on her lips.

"You're right, you haven't. If I give you my name it destroys the mysterious aura I have."

She rolled her eyes, a smile still on her face as she shook her head.

"Well, how about I tell you my name first?"

"If you insist."

She suddenly looked nervous to tell me. Her shoulders were rigid and her mouth was set in a tight line, as if she was worried it would ruin the night if we knew anything else about each other. At first, I thought she must have the worst name in the world based on how painful it seemed for her to tell me. But then, she exhaled slowly and whispered, "Maren."

I've definitely heard worse names. I liked Maren, it suited her at least. So far, it seemed like she wasn't exactly like Jade or Allie, but maybe a mix of them? *I'm not sure, I guess I'll have to find out more.*

"Maren is much better than Sam," I said. Her eyes dilated a little bit at that.

"Sam is your name?" she asked.

I nodded with a slow gulp of my drink, the whisky burning the back of my throat.

She eyed the glass; the condensation of the water kept dripping on the tablecloth, and while she tried to keep eye contact with me, she kept diverting back down toward it. I offered her a sip, which she denied at first. I shrugged and kept my fingers around the glass, swirling the whisky around as I held it out slightly to her. I could see her wanting to cave in and take a few long gulps of it. Not that I could blame her. After the night she'd had, she needed more than just a few sips. She reluctantly took it from my hands, nearly downing the contents inside, before she set it carefully back into my hand.

"Do you want a drink? Or maybe we could get a dessert?" I asked.

"Could we get both?" A blush slowly spanned her cheeks as she asked sheepishly. "Unless you've got somewhere to be?"

I shook my head and flagged down the waiter, ordering more whisky and chocolate lava cake for the both of us. She drank the whisky rather quickly, all of it going straight to her head as she almost missed her mouth with the few bites of chocolate cake she had. Like most of the food we had tonight, the cake didn't shape up any better.

After a few bites she dropped her fork, whispering, "Does this cake taste weird to you?"

I set my fork to the side as well, pushing the nauseating plate to the side as I replied, "I'm not sure how they messed it up this bad."

She chuckled and wiped her mouth with her napkin, a small red lipstick stain remaining on it.

I motioned my head to the door. "Wanna get out of here?"

She nodded, and I paid a few minutes later. We stood up and walked to the front where she stumbled more than I thought she would. It was clear that she was tipsy, with that big never-ending goofy grin on her face and several near-twistings of her ankles. It obviously didn't take much for her to get a buzz going. *Good to know.*

I stared up at the sky, trying to look philosophical or some shit. She seemed like she fed off that stuff, because soon enough her head was tilted, trying to give off that same impression. She linked her arm with mine, getting a little too cozy with someone she had just met, but that could've been the alcohol or her lack of judgment about someone. Either way, I didn't mind. We strolled along the sidewalk, passing numerous happy couples while we were only pretending to be one. We got overly warm and friendly eyes from the older couples or nods from the younger ones, and towards the end, I could tell she was missing her ex-boyfriend with each glance we got and how quiet she had become.

Thankfully, we landed upon a cluster of food trucks, and her mood switched instantly. My stomach growled as we reached them; the shitty, gristle-filled steak had done nothing for me other than increase my bill after I reluctantly added hers as well. We ordered from a taco truck. The others were mostly vegan, and while they probably had decent food, tofu nuggets just looked unappetizing to me. We sat on a bench a few feet over and ate the soft-shelled chicken tacos, spilling some of the juices onto my shirt and her dress with each bite.

I glanced over to see her take a rather large bite, trying to finish the taco to prevent any more stains on her tan dress. She saw me staring and goofily smiled. "I didn't expect these to be so messy." She wiped off some sauce from her mouth with the sleeve of her dress, seemingly forgoing the thought of trying to keep it clean.

I shrugged. "We are a little overdressed for a taco truck."

She nodded and set her trash to the side. "You make a good point there." She paused, looking down at her feet, while she said, "Thanks for cheering me up and paying for dinner tonight."

"Don't worry about it. I had a great time, despite the circumstances."

She smiled; another blush coated her cheeks. She blushed more than any person I had ever seen. But to be fair, she did have really pale skin.

"Aaron never liked paying for anything," she said.

I leaned back on the bench, wrapping my arm loosely around her shoulder. "Well, that was your first mistake."

She whipped her head in my direction before replying, "What do you mean?"

"Dating a guy named Aaron. That was your first mistake." I winked, nudging her in the side. She rolled her eyes and slapped my arm playfully.

"I suppose you're right, never liked his name anyway." She giggled as she leaned her head on my shoulder.

"Surprised you dated him that long if you hated his name that much."

"Is there some judgment I hear in your voice?" she said playfully, as she raised her head back up, her green eyes pooling into mine.

"No, not at all, trust me. I was in the same situation you were."

"Hated your girlfriend's name?" she asked teasingly.

I shrugged. "I mean, Cassie wasn't my favorite name, but I probably wasn't as bothered with it as much as you were. But I meant being in a relationship I shouldn't have been in."

"Couldn't agree more." A sad smile reached her face before she shook it off. I looked down at my watch and my eyes widened when I noticed it was already nearly midnight.

"I should probably get you back home, didn't realize it was so late."

She looked down at her phone, also checking the time.

"Yeah, I should probably get back."

Her apartment was only a few blocks over, thankfully, both of us too bloated from the shitty restaurant food and the messy but satisfying taco.

"So, am I going to hear from you again?" she asked, as we reached the stairs of her building. I liked how she took charge. I mean, it was clear she wanted someone to help her get over her ex, but I didn't mind.

"Do you want to?" I leaned in closer to her, and small puffs of her breath hit my neck. She was much shorter than I was and had to crane her neck to meet my eyes.

"Only if you want to," she replied, trying not to seem too eager. She took a few steps back, looking like she felt empowered by the fact that she left me wondering, wanting.

I gave her my number, much to her satisfaction. A small smile played on her lips as she hung around the door.

"Will you actually call me?" she yelled after I waved goodbye, when I was a few steps down the road already.

"Guess you'll find out!" I yelled back and winked, even though she probably didn't see it. I turned back around, a smirk growing on my face as I knew she was still hovering by the door, watching me walk away.

Cassie

You know, I wasn't sure if I was ever gonna reach back out to her again. But when I saw her walking across the street from me, towards her apartment building, I felt like I needed to talk to her again.

She instantly saw me and rolled her eyes, slamming the door in front of me as she strolled up the stairs of her apartment building. She always did this, not letting me speak my mind while she was able to do so whenever, whether that was verbally or by slamming the door.

I knocked on the door, thoroughly pissed off but trying to soften my face to hopefully get her to change her mind. Thankfully, I was successful. I saw her externally huff and make her way back down. Her eyes were hard, and her mouth was set in a firm line. It was clear she wore her emotions on her face, and I was not someone she wanted to speak with, let alone look at today.

She unlocked the door, opening it just a crack to hear me.

"What do you want, Sam?" She shifted on her feet, adjusting a backpack on her back that looked heavy.

"Can we talk?"

She looked at her watch. "Little late, huh? What has it been, like two months?"

"Six weeks," I answered, and she gave me a pointed look. "Just for a few minutes?"

She sighed and cracked the door open further, letting me slide through as she turned back towards the stairs. "Five. I've gotta head over to a pottery class soon."

I nodded, although she couldn't see me. She threw open her door and set her backpack down on a plush chair. She strolled over to the fridge and pulled out two Cokes and tossed one to me before sitting down on her couch.

"How have you been?" I asked.

"Don't do that. No small talk. If you were actually interested in knowing, you would've come back sooner than now." She was blunt, one of the reasons that drew me to her when we first met. She denied me at first, and made me work for it for a few weeks before she finally gave in. And now, she was giving me the same cold stare as she did when I first approached her months ago.

"Fair enough. I want to get back together."

She scoffed and took a long sip of her Coke before setting it on the side table. "Get back together," she repeated, chuckling dryly. "Took you a while to realize that, didn't it?"

I almost spoke up before she continued on. She stood up to pace as she did often when she was frustrated.

"Sam, you were the one to break it off! You knew where I lived, where I worked, hell... you even had a key that I forgot to get back. Why are you doing this now?"

"I fucked up, okay? I know that. And trust me, I've tried to come by for weeks now, but I was afraid that it would end up like this." I scratched the back of my neck.

She pulled a pillow to her chest and clung to it tightly, as if that pillow was helping her compose herself. "Sam I can't just wait around for you anymore. I'm twenty-six now. All my friends are either married, having kids, or in long-term relationships. I'm sick of being with guys that don't know what they want."

"I know you are. I remember you telling me that when we first started dating. I know what I want now, and that's you."

I could see her chest rapidly rising and falling, and that pillow didn't seem to be giving her any comfort whatsoever.

"I appreciate that, Sam. Can I take some time to think about it?"

"Of course." I stood up along with her, wiping my sweaty palms onto my jeans as we walked towards the door. She had a small smile on her face, her hand resting on the door. It looked like she wanted to say something but instead she held her tongue. I sighed and laid against the door after she closed it. *Seems like it'll take a little more convincing.*

I could never tell if she was lying. She liked to have her own independence and alone time, and I wanted to make sure she hadn't met another guy. She was pretty enough to get a guy whenever she wanted, so I stayed behind the stoop of her apartment, waiting for her to leave, to see where she was going. And, like she said, she went to that pottery class. Her hair was in a messy bun with some dried clay on her hands, jeans, and on her face, but she didn't seem to mind. She returned home after that, relaxing in front of the TV with her feet propped up on the coffee table. She should honestly shut her blinds more.

The next day, I kept checking my phone, feeling the phantom buzzing of the texts and calls she never sent in my pocket as I walked around town. She was never quick to make a decision, either, which was one of the reasons I ended it with her. But after talking with those other girls, I came to realize it wasn't just Cassie who was indecisive; it was nearly the whole damn population. But I hoped, when it came to us, she would move faster than this.

So, later in the afternoon, I checked in on her. She went back to that pottery place, Clay Heaven, close to her apartment. I could tell she had developed this into a hobby after we broke up, since dozens of half-broken, multicolored little vases and pots encompassed the random spots of that apartment. By the look of those pots and vases, this was a hobby she should probably give up.

Anyway, she left carrying another vase in her hand. She had probably wasted hundreds of dollars in there. I'll never understand why anyone spends money attempting to make half-assed mugs, but she clearly enjoyed wasting her money there.

Either way, she was much more predictable than she thought she was. I only dated her for eight months and I could pick up on all of that. She'd go to work each morning, teaching middle-aged moms how to do yoga, around 8 a.m., putting on a preppy face as she'd teach them difficult poses. Each mother would arrive in overpriced, bright athletic wear and flick some water on their face after the class was done to appear like they actually could perform the poses, when in reality, all of those mothers could barely touch their toes and it showed. Cassie seemed to like it, despite that she would get the same boring crowd every day, and would leave to go on to her next job.

She didn't believe in working the usual 9-5 workday, and she made every effort to prevent that by having two barely-above-minimum-wage jobs to support herself. This job was a change of pace and was a bookstore a few blocks over. Her shifts there weren't nearly as long, and they always seemed to fly by quickly. Then, after a short shift, she'd plop herself down on her couch and mentally prepare herself for the next day.

Despite the predictability aspect that she clearly hadn't realized about herself, there were a lot of qualities that I did like about her. Smart, witty, annoying, but charming. And it wasn't until I saw her again that I realized that I was really just trying to find someone like her.

I thought I could get closer to the other girls, and to some extent I did. I tried to get to know them, set them apart from her, but at the end of each night, I would stare at her number on my screen, not theirs.

And now, I had been giving her a week. I thought that should be enough time, despite her indecisiveness. At first, I thought it was because she was too busy that week; she had never liked technology and even hated texting or calling her friends.

But then I saw her at the bar with a few of her friends, hair pulled back in a tight ponytail that matched the tight low-cut dress she had on, flirting with other guys who tried to make a pass at her. She even played into it a bit. Or I watched her as she went out to dinner with her friend, Dylan, who always seemed like more than a friend, to me. How can you be best friends for nearly fifteen years and not have anything going on between you?

The rest of the nights, she sprawled on the couch with that cat she got two weeks after we broke up, supposedly. She knew I was allergic to them, so she must've gotten it to spite me.

After that, I got the hint.

It didn't really matter how many days I gave her; her decision would still be the same: not to get back together.

I was the first guy she dated in nearly three years and we only lasted eight months. I could see why.

When I finally talked to her, it wasn't at the studio, bookstore, or pottery shop. It was in the small parking garage that was connected to her apartment building. She never drove anywhere. She liked the environment a little too much and would bike and walk everywhere, even to her two jobs. So, whenever she would twirl those car keys around her fingers, I knew she was planning to go far. She was probably heading to Dylan's house. He lived around 40 minutes away, and she always went there more than I liked. She would use that as an excuse as to why we couldn't hang out, because she needed to see him. Despite the fact that I hadn't seen her in a week when she saw him the other day. She did that a lot. And, knowing her, she was going to do it this time again. I couldn't let her have that excuse again. Not anymore.

She was getting into her little beat-up Volkswagen when she saw me. Instantly she rolled her eyes as I made my way over to the driver's side.

"What are you doing here?" she asked.

"Really, Cassie? It's been over a week."

"Did my silence not give you your answer?

"I'd like to talk about this," I urged.

"I'm not talking about this now. I'm late."

"Going over to Dylan's then?"

"What's that got to do anything?" she spat, her face reddening as she gripped her steering wheel tighter, her leg blocking her from closing her door.

"You only drive when you go see him."

She scoffed, ignoring my statement. "I'll see you later, Sam."

She moved her leg into the car and went to slam the car door before I blocked it with my hand.

Names

I definitely think I was just trying to find someone like Cassie. She's infuriating, but I'm sure you gathered that rather quickly. I thought I could make it work with her, but she was never transparent. I'm sure you picked up on that, too. Dylan was much more than a friend, and I think she wanted to disregard it, keep it in the back of her mind, and use him as a backup if she needed. While, in retrospect, it was the guys that she actually dated that were consistently on the back burner. I knew she'd figure it out eventually, and realize how wrong and selfish it was of her to do that.

I thought I could replace her with Jade. She seemed promising at first. A real spitfire, not afraid to speak her mind. She didn't resemble her at all in appearance. With Jade being a dirty blonde, fake with hair extensions and exceptionally long clumpy eyelashes, I was surprised I even considered her in the first place. Now that I'm thinking about it, it could've been her cold demeanor, how you could tell she was itching for a fight, an excuse to attack and belittle someone verbally, which I'm sure she's been wanting to do for years. Anyway, I suppose that's what got me interested in Jade: not her stark contrast of appearance to Cassie, but her will to speak her mind, regardless of the feelings of others.

Now, Allie was a different story entirely. I liked her innocence, her vulnerability. Not in a creepy way, though. Just in the way that I could tell she needed someone to rely on, and not to rely so much on herself anymore. I guess she looked like Cassie to a certain extent, sporting the same brunette hair, and a little too many layers that resembled Rachel from *Friends*, but she still looked like her in a few ways. With her, I liked the challenge of trying to find out more about her and get her to open up without pushing her too far. She was a lot like Cassie in that way, not wanting to open up, and then doing so not too long after.

But I have to say, I wasn't expecting Maren. I honestly was just having dinner at that shitty restaurant, and she happened to fall into my lap. Literally. I also didn't expect to pay more than 50 bucks that night, but I couldn't *not* pay for her food, right? At least I was being nice there, I debated not paying for it, but her mascara-smudged eyes turned my heart around. I liked her eagerness, even though she was so hell-bent on not trying to show it. She was driven and had initiative. Something that Cassie clearly lacked.

Ultimately though, I guess I just wanted to have Cassie back. I shouldn't have broken up with her in the first place. I was just being petty, not liking her constant driving to Dylan's house, the annoying slurping of her drinks, or random sighs in an otherwise quiet apartment for no reason. It was all little things. But I can't hone in on those anymore. I'm 27. Which is hard to believe. But like she said, we both can't be waiting around for someone better; they come few and far between at our age. Not that I'm saying not to be picky and follow the "guidelines" that you set up for yourself when critiquing people to date, but maybe don't be as picky as I am.

It's not Cassie, she's not the one. I realize that now. But I'm not sure it's those three women, either. Maybe I just need to start fresh, meet other women, and not compare to them to Cassie like I did with Allie, Jade, and Maren. There's someone else out there for me, but first, I gotta figure out how to get rid of Cassie.

Once she's gone, I'll be able to move on.

CHAPTER 13
Letters

I have been writing letters to my grandma for a little over a year now. I've yet to meet her, but I was tired of my mom dictating whether or not I could talk to her. You guessed it: they had a falling out a few years before I was born, and because of that, my mother has never brought me around to her or had my grandma visit. I resorted to looking up her address, and began writing weekly letters to her ever since.

She seemed ecstatic in the first letter and wanted to know all about me. To be honest, I was surprised that she hadn't wanted to come over and meet me and mend her relationship with my mom (considering our address was on each letter), but I didn't press it. I just figured she didn't want to make things worse with my mom.

At the end of each letter, I'd plead with her to come visit and would tell her that everything that happened between her and my mom was water under the bridge. I knew that it wasn't, but I figured that if they had a big screaming match with one another, they'd make up and finally get rid of this long-standing grudge.

Finally, it worked. I convinced my grandma to visit. When she was set to arrive, I couldn't help but feel a mix of jitters and an overwhelming sense of excitement. It's always been just me and my mom, and meeting other members of my family was a dream come true.

I didn't think anything could break my spirit until I heard my mom scream my name. She was standing over my desk, one of the letters in her hand. I sucked in a breath, realizing that I forgot to put it away. She turned to me with a raised eyebrow.

"What is this?" she asked, crumpling the paper slightly in her hand.

I took a calming breath. "Please don't get mad. I've been writing letters to grandma."

My mom redirected her focus to the paper, her eyes taking in the cursive handwriting of my grandma. "Honey, this isn't from your grandma."

My heart dropped in my stomach. "What do you mean?"

"First of all, this isn't her handwriting. But more importantly, this isn't her address. She moved several years ago." Realization dawned on her features as she read over the last line: the line where my supposed grandma told me when she'd arrive at our house.

"Did you tell this person to come over? Honey, why would you do that?"

"All the kids in class talk about their grandparents, and I just wanted to be able to talk to mine, get to know my grandma. Is that so wrong?"

My mom put a hand on her forehead, taking a deep breath. "I understand that, I do, but there is a reason why I don't talk to her. Why I don't want her in our lives."

"That's not fair, Mom. Why can't I be the judge of that?"

“Look, I’m not getting into this right now, okay? I will tell you my reasoning once we’ve calmed down a bit. But for now, you just gave someone our address. Who knows who this sicko is? This person has been pretending to be Grandma, we’ve gotta--”

She was interrupted by three loud knocks on the door. Mom looked at me, all color drained from her face.

The door rattled with louder knocks, knocks that an old lady wouldn’t be able to make.

CHAPTER 14
Grief in Parts

D*iscovering*

I found out about the cancer when my mother was bedridden in the hospital. By the look on her face, I gathered she didn't even want to tell me, but she had to, seeing that she had an oxygen mask and an IV hanging beside her.

I knew I'd lose my mom earlier than most; she was 45 when she had me. But I didn't expect it to be a few months after starting my freshman year of college at NYU.

My 9 a.m. class was a few minutes in, and I had a death grip on my coffee. I drank it as fast I could, burning my tastebuds in an attempt to rejuvenate myself quickly. I took a long blink before the vibration of my phone woke me back up, and I squinted to see my mother's picture staring back at me. I narrowed my eyes, knowing she wouldn't be calling without a reason. I haphazardly shoved my things into my backpack and ran out of the lecture hall, picking up breathlessly on the last ring.

"What's up, Mom?"

"Hi, is this Harper?" The woman on the phone asked. My breath hitched and I barely managed to squeak out a response.

"Umm, yes this is."

"Hi, Harper. I am one of your mother's nurses down at Denver Health..."

I drowned out the rest, before somehow managing to quickly book the last seat on the first flight back to Colorado.

I rushed back to my dorm, throwing as many clothes as I could in my suitcase before heading to the airport. The nurse didn't tell me much, other than I needed to get there as soon as possible, which didn't necessarily help with my fear of planes. There had only been a handful of times during my childhood when my mother had gotten a cold or the flu; I had a gut feeling this was worse, since the nurse wouldn't tell me what was going on.

I wasn't originally going to go to NYU. In fact, my mother had to convince me to go. If you couldn't gather by now, my mom and I are incredibly close, similar to Lorelai and Rory Gilmore's relationship. I hadn't spent much time--or any, really-- away from my mom, so to live in a whole other state? It wasn't even a consideration.

It was, however, something that my mother pined for. She attended NYU, and seeing as how I wanted to be a writer, it seemed fitting. But for the entire plane ride home, all I could think about was how I wished I was closer.

A few hours later, I stood outside the automatic doors of the hospital, afraid of what I'd see when I arrived at her room. At reception, I asked for her name, and then embarked on the confusing journey to her room. It involved so many twists and turns that I'm surprised I even was able to find it. I read the plaque--Room 4052--took a big breath in, and rounded the corner to her room. Frankly, it still didn't register in my mind that she was even sick until I saw her lying in that hospital bed, with so many tubes and wires I could barely see her under them.

I walked over to the side of her bed and sat down in the chair next to it, thankful there was a chair, as I felt like my legs could collapse at any moment. She was asleep, though based on the pained, contorted look on her face, it didn't seem peaceful whatsoever. I blinked away a few tears that formed, reached for her hand, and gave it a tiny squeeze, which accidentally woke her up. Her piercing blue eyes seemed duller somehow as she focused her eyes on me, a small smile forming underneath the oxygen mask. With her other hand, she smoothed out her hair out of habit, surely feeling out of her element. She usually had her perfect greying hair in a new style, instead of the mess it was on the pillow.

I tried pulling my hand from hers, afraid that it would be too much for her, but she held on as tight as she could. I knew she wasn't up for being badgered with a million questions, but I couldn't help myself from asking, "Why didn't you tell me?"

She took off her oxygen mask, her lips white as a sheet. "I didn't know how...t-to tell you."

"How bad is it?"

My mom sighed and looked away from me for a second before responding, "Stage four."

I gasped, let go of her hand, and stood up quickly. I paced around the room while she watched, not saying a word, as I tried to process this as fast as I could. "When did you start treatments? Are they helping?"

"I haven't had any treatments, honey."

My shoes scuffed the floor from stopping abruptly, which made my mom wince. *Why hasn't she done any treatments?*

"What do you mean? We could've paid for the treatments, Mom. We have all that money you saved for my college."

She instantly shook her head at this statement. "That money is yours."

"Maybe we can still fight this."

She sighed, looking as though she wished she could escape from this conversation as much as I did. "I don't want to do that. I sure as hell don't want to be hooked up to machines, withering away for whatever time I have left. I certainly don't want you seeing me like that..." She took a big, pained breath in before continuing, "I've lived a great life, honey, and I know you'll have a great life without me. I just wish I could be in it longer."

She died at 7:03 p.m., only a few hours after I learned about the cancer. Between one of my inconsolable sobbing fits, the nurse who called me took me to a bereavement room to talk next steps.

"I know this is hard, but I need to ask this. Do you know if she wanted to be buried or cremated?"

A wave of nausea washed over me at this question, which the nurse seemed to notice, and she gave me a cup of water.

"Cremated, I think," I replied.

"Okay. I only have a few more questions, Harper." I nodded and answered the best I could, but I was lost in my own world.

As the nurse wrapped up the questions, she gave me a contact for a grief counselor and my mom's belongings before I walked out of the hospital. By the time I left, it was approaching 10 p.m. and was freezing outside. Luckily I had my winter coat, as my car was at my mom's house and I didn't necessarily want to cry in an Uber. The four-mile trek home was long, especially with having to drag my suitcase behind me, and I couldn't feel a thing, which was partly because of the cold and because I didn't want to.

Sometime later, I stood in the driveway, a million thoughts running through my mind, but the main one was how weird it felt to walk into her house without her. I pushed them aside, feeling exhaustion creeping up on me as I slowly walked to the front door and unlocked it.

I flipped the light switch on and nearly jumped when I heard Marty's paws hit the floor as he sprinted towards me. He wiggled around for a few minutes as I petted him, before he took me to his empty food bowl. I filled it to the brim and spilled some on the floor, as his impatience caused me to drop the bag. I bent down to clean up the mess, but seeing as he had already scarfed down the majority of his food within seconds, I decided to leave it and head to bed. What would mom have done with Marty? Would she have given him to our neighbors until I got back? Or did she not think that far?

I collapsed into my childhood bed moments later, and my cries filled the silent house for the rest of the night.

The Empty House

I never had a longing to have a sibling until that moment. I was quite content with it just being me and my mom , and maybe for selfish reasons, I liked being an only child because I got all of the attention. But now, in this quiet house, I wished I had someone else to share this grief with.

I hadn't navigated death before, so when I woke up the next morning, my face dry with streaks of tears, I forgot she was even gone. Marty was asleep on the bed beside me, so I carefully slid out of the covers and headed to the living room, before catching a light that was still on in my mom's bedroom. I couldn't bring myself to go into her room the night before, so I didn't even notice it. I managed to take a few steps toward the room and stopped at the doorway. My eyes teared up at how normal her room looked, as if she'd be coming back to it. Her bed was unmade, though it was most of the time, and she had clothes folded neatly into stacks on the floor with some dirty clothes thrown haphazardly into the hamper. She also had a half-drunk coffee sitting on her nightstand. I quickly took the cup into the kitchen to wash, as I no longer was able to spend another second in there. It was in a mug that I had made her in one of my art classes at school. It was nothing special, a turquoise and blue mixture of colors with the rim slightly lopsided, but there was never a morning where I didn't see her drink from it. Despite having her cabinets filled to the brim with other mugs, she only used that one.

After the mug dried, I placed it back where it belonged and tidied up the rest of the house as best as I could, still wanting to feel her presence there and not disrupt the house too much.

My mom bought this quaint, two-bedroom house a few months after I was born. The sole purpose of her buying this house was because it's on the same street as the elementary school. She'd always tell me that she wanted to walk me to school and home from school every day like her mom used to, and this house was perfect for that. We'd get up a few minutes early every day and would make the walk over, rain or shine.

While I would grow annoyed at walking in the rain with a flimsy umbrella on the way to school, or stepping through several inches of snow, I couldn't imagine growing up in any other house. Every couple of months, the house would change in some shape or form; my mom would either grow tired of the paint covering the walls, or would buy a new decoration to spruce it up.

My mom would pick out a new lively paint, whether that was a bright purple or green, and we'd paint for hours on whatever wall she wanted updated. After that, we'd spend hours in a Home Goods and shove things into the cart to redecorate. Because of this, our house was pretty cluttered, seeing as Mom rarely parted with any of the hundreds of decorations we bought over the years.

And while I used to love walking around our house and remembering those moments of being splattered with paint, or placing our newly-bought decorations in the best spot within the house, standing in this house now made me realize that she was what made our house a home.

And now it's just empty.

The Visitors

The next few days were a blur, really. I'd wake up and the day would pass by in the blink of an eye. The only thing I would accomplish was getting a shower and microwaving up some nasty frozen meal.

I had stumbled upon my mom's liquor cabinet three nights after she passed. Well, it wasn't a cabinet, but an old credenza at the far end of the kitchen. It was my grandmother's, and I hardly saw my mom around it, apart from occasionally dusting it. Around midnight, I grew curious about what was inside it, since when I was growing up my mom told me not to go near it. I always chalked that up to her not wanting the credenza to somehow get broken. Nevertheless, I carefully opened up the doors and saw several bottles of wine stashed inside. My eyes widened, as I had never seen her drink a sip of alcohol, but I suppose she would drink a glass or two after I went to bed.

I ended up grabbing the bottle closest to me and nearly drank all of it, but I stopped when the room became fuzzy. I laid down a few minutes later, not even bothering to take off my clothes, and closed my eyes. I felt Marty lay down beside me, and I fell asleep within seconds.

The next morning, with more than a slight hangover, I decided to venture to the living room instead of lying in my bed all day. I was halfway in between my first movie of the day when a curt knock interrupted. I narrowed my eyes at Marty and whispered, "Who do you think is at the door? Should I ignore them?"

If it wasn't for Marty's barking at these questions I would've just stayed on the couch, but after another round of knocking, I made my way towards the door and flung it open.

Standing there was a man in a navy-blue suit with a bright pink tie, towering over me. He looked down as I stared at him.

"Hi?" I greeted, though it sounded more like a question.

"Hi. I was just wondering if Betty was here?"

My heart dropped, and I immediately felt nauseous. For a few seconds, I thought about lying, saying that she was out of town for a couple of days, rather than saying she passed away. It seemed simpler and much easier to say, but it would catch up to me, and I'd have to confront the fact that she isn't coming back.

"Who are you?" I asked instead. I propped the door open even further, letting in the cold air.

"I'm Russ Banks. I'm her boss."

"Oh, I'm her daughter, Harper. Would you like to come in?"

"If I could, please."

I asked if he wanted a cup of coffee and he politely declined, but he did sit down on the couch instead. I took a big breath, trying to keep my tears at bay, and I told him of my mother's sudden passing.

He sucked in a breath at the news, and his face suddenly turned from confusion to sympathy. “I’m so sorry to hear that, Harper. I didn’t even know she was sick.”

I was tempted to say that I didn’t know either, but instead, I gave a curt nod. An awkward silence ensued, but after a minute or two, I piped up with, “I’m thankful that she had such a caring boss like you. Thanks for checking up on her.”

He smiled, and told me to check in with him at any time. When he was halfway out the door, I stopped him with, “Did you know that out of all the jobs she had, this was her favorite?”

He smiled once more. “I didn’t know that.”

“She always talked about how great of a boss you were, and I’m not just saying that. She’d tell me all the time. But anyway, it’s nice to put a face to the name.”

He looked like he blushed at this, although with how cold it was, it was hard to tell. He chatted for a few minutes after, and gave me a long but awkward hug before I closed the door. I slid down it, though I misjudged the distance, and fell hard on the floor, pain shooting through my hips.

I managed to crawl to the couch and stayed there for the rest of the day, rounding out the overall shitty day by watching one of my mom’s favorite movies, *Pitch Perfect*. She had always been a musical fan, and even joined an acapella group in college, so she dragged me to the theaters several times. And then, when it came out on DVD, there wasn’t a weekend where we wouldn’t watch it. I knew that as soon as I scrolled through our collection of DVDs, I needed to watch it. Until bed, I kept the movie on replay, wanting to drown out the otherwise overwhelming sound of silence that filled the house. I ended up falling asleep near midnight on the couch, and headed to bed shortly after. Once again, Marty crawled in and laid down beside me. Despite being exhausted out in the living room, I suddenly had a new sense of energy, and started thinking about the interaction with my mom's boss. I hadn't even thought of contacting anyone yet, and I sat up at the realization that I hadn't even contacted any of my professors since she passed.

I pulled my email up on my laptop and took a shaky breath in, not realizing how daunting it would be to draft these emails. Now I could no longer pretend that the last few days hadn't happened, and I had to face the reality that either I needed to not go back this semester, or I needed to start making the drive back. Somehow I managed to send the emails through blurry eyes and closed my laptop shut, my head pounding from the bright screen light. Sleep evaded me as I tossed and turned all night, and I only fell asleep into a deep slumber in the early hours of the morning, which was conveniently when Marty started barking for food.

I rolled out of bed with a huff and glanced at my laptop on my desk. I was tempted to see if my professors responded, but with Marty's impatient tug on my pant leg, I held off. I went along with the rest of my morning, and opened up my laptop again in the midafternoon. I didn't realize that I had missed over a week of classes until the emails from my professors pointed it out.

Some were kinder than others, giving me extensions on assignments, while others expressed no sympathy whatsoever and told me that if I didn't submit all of my past-due assignments within a week, they had no choice but to fail me. I closed my laptop angrily, puzzled about what to do next.

"You don't think I should go back, do you?" Marty didn't even look in my direction when I asked this, or my follow-up question, "Do you think Mom would be disappointed if I dropped out this semester?"

Almost as a way to show disapproval, Marty walked out of the room. I decided to schedule an appointment with my academic advisor to figure out my options.

“Are you returning to finish out this fall semester?” Jane, my advisor, asked. We were on a Zoom call, talking about my next steps, when I shook my head at this question.

“I was thinking of taking a gap year instead and returning next year in the fall. Can I do that?”

“You certainly can, if you feel like that would work better for you?” She asked it as a question despite trying to make it a statement. “But if you are going to withdraw for the semester then you’ll need to pack up your dorm room, and apply for housing again next fall.”

I felt relief when I closed my laptop after that conversation, although that quickly faltered when I heard the doorbell ring. I opened the door to Shelley, one of the neighbors a few doors down, holding a casserole dish.

“Hi, Shelley. What brings you on by?”

Shelley shivered despite wearing a thick coat and replied, “Hi, honey. I wanted to check in on how you were doing and express my condolences. You know how much we loved your mother...” She tapered off as she saw my tearful reaction.

Shelley has lived in this neighborhood longer than my mom and I have. She’s experienced her first marriage, kids, divorce, and second marriage all in that one house. And she is one of the nosiest people you’ll ever meet. I was surprised that she hadn’t popped by earlier, considering my mom and her talked almost every day, but I supposed she was just giving me time.

“I appreciate that, Shelley.”

I glanced down at the casserole, and she smiled and said, “I made this for you. All you gotta do is pop it in the oven to warm it up.” She passed me the heavy dish, and I thanked her. “Well, I won’t keep you, but please don't hesitate to reach out to me if you need anything, okay?"

She started making her way down the driveway before I stopped her.

"Actually, I was hoping to ask you for a favor."

Shelley ended up taking Marty home with her a couple of minutes after I explained I needed to retrieve my things at the dorm. I spent the next few days driving to New York and hated every second of it. Normally, I didn't mind long car rides, especially since I had grown accustomed to them with my mom on our trips. But all I could do was think about my last interaction with her. I know she had her reasons for not telling me, but I'd still rather have known, perhaps to talk her into treatment, or even just to give me more time to process her imminent death.

I glanced down at the steering wheel, my knuckles white from gripping it so tight. I didn't realize that I harbored pent-up anger towards my mom, but instead of diving into why I felt that way, I decided to think about something else. Well, I tried not to think much at all, really, but when you're sitting in silence for 26 hours, it's inevitable. I spent the rest of the drive either bawling my eyes out or fuming.

When I finally arrived at the dorm, I hesitated at the door for a few seconds. *Should I knock, or just barge in?* Technically it was my room, but it almost didn't feel like it at the same time. I ended up knocking on the door and my roommate, Brooke, softly replied, "Come in!"

I took a big breath in and opened the door. Brooke was sitting on her bed, looking at her laptop, before locking eyes with mine. As soon as she started rolling out of bed to greet me, I broke down. She wrapped me up in a tight hug while I tried to calm down, though that took a while. She didn't complain about her tear-stained shirt when I sat down next to her on my bed, and she didn't interrupt when I spilled everything about the last couple of weeks that I'd had. She listened for well over an hour, until my grumbling stomach interjected.

"Want to grab some dinner?" she asked, a small smile on her face.

I nodded, and soon after, we ended up in a pizza restaurant that's just a few minutes from our dorm. We went there our fair share in the nearly two months we lived together, and I hated that I wouldn't be here for these moments anymore. I lucked out with Brooke as a roommate, but I knew in my gut I needed time to sort out my life, and figure out how to move on without my mom. I couldn't waste the money my mom saved up and worked so hard for by staying and getting terrible grades.

Brooke promised to stay in touch as she helped me shove my things into boxes, and even though I grew teary-eyed at times while packing up my stuff, I knew it was for the best.

The Holiday Season

I found the costume my mother was supposed to wear for Halloween hanging up in her closet. It was halfway done, and truthfully it looked like a hodge-podge of random fabrics somewhat strewn together, rather than an actual costume. I have no idea what she was trying to make, but I do know that this was my mom's favorite holiday. It was going to be the first Halloween we'd spend apart, I had actually booked a plane ticket to surprise her, but you see how that turned out.

I didn't bother with decorations for a few reasons, but mainly because I forgot they were stored in the shed outside, and I didn't want to venture out there. To make up for it, I ended up buying heaps of candy so that when I set the bowl outside instead of handing it out I wouldn't be bombarded too much. Well, at least, that's what I hoped. Within the first few parties of trick-or-treaters, the doorbell rang.

Despite wanting to ignore it, I answered anyway, and was met with Iron Man, a butterfly, and a kid who appeared to be dressed as a duck.

"Where's Betty?" Iron Man asked with a slight head tilt.

"Oh, umm... she's out of town," I lied, but saw no need to tell him the truth at the moment. He nodded and grabbed a handful of candy before heading over to the next house.

My plan to keep the bowl outside for the remainder of the night was ruined by the waves of kids that never stopped coming for hours. After the last round of kids, I flopped down on my bed, more exhausted than I anticipated, though I appreciated not having to think about my mom and her excitement at wearing whatever costume she was making.

For the better part of a month, most of my days after that dreadful holiday consisted of staying on the couch--much to Marty's delight, seeing that he's always been a couch potato. I'd occasionally walk on my mother's treadmill when my back would start hurting from laying in the same position on the couch, but since it was in her room, I didn't like to do that often. This routine spilled into Thanksgiving, which in my house was never a day spent hovering over the oven.

If there's one thing you should know about my mom, it's that she couldn't cook. For Thanksgiving, we'd normally order takeout, snuggle up on the couch, and watch movies together. But this year, I decided to cook. Yes, I'd have a lot of leftovers, but at least making a massive meal would take my mind off things and I wouldn't have to cook for a few days. My mom had a dusty cookbook full of recipes that I wanted to attempt, so I blew off the excessive amounts of dust caked on those pages and searched for an easy-to-make recipe with few ingredients.

I didn't want a big turkey by myself, so I bought a small rotisserie chicken instead. With it, I made a sweet potato casserole, dumplings, and pecan pie; nothing too fancy. But I was able to eat the leftovers for days, so that was a plus. I ate the food on the couch, which was a little hard, since I filled my plate to the brim. I put on *It's a Charlie Brown Thanksgiving,* one of my mom's favorites, as I took food coma naps and snuggled with Marty.

I tried to get excited for Christmas, but I knew it wouldn't measure up. About two months after her death, just a little over a week until Christmas, I suddenly realized this would be the first Christmas without her. I was able to get through Halloween and Thanksgiving with only shedding a few tears, but now it was truly setting in how much she was missing, and how much I missed her.

I couldn't get my mind off the traditions we'd have, like making new ornaments each year and hanging them on the tree. I wasn't too crafty, but my mom sure was. She didn't like using the plain old traditional ornaments, so we'd make new ones to add to our pile and overwhelm the tree. By the time I was almost finished decorating the tree, I glanced down at the box and noticed I had barely made a dent in the pile of ornaments. I reached down and picked up the first one we made together. We ended up wrapping a picture of us around the ornament; I couldn't have been any older than five, and she looked young without all of her grey hairs.

On top of the homemade ornaments, my mom always wanted us to make one homemade gift for each other. She was much more creative than me, and could whip something up within an hour, while I usually had to start thinking of ideas in June. I loved having a simple Christmas with her every year. We could add or take away traditions, which we did often. Then, we'd make the four-hour drive over to my aunt's house and spend time with her family.

I needed to call my Aunt Linda. I hadn't really heard from her since my mom passed away, other than a simple text the next day of how sorry she was and she hoped I was doing okay. I wasn't, but replied that I was hanging in there and would love a visit from her and my cousins, but she never replied.

I pulled out my phone, my hands shaking as I dialed her number, hoping they weren't going on vacation this year like they did last. The phone rang a few times before my aunt's hoarse voice from smoking too many cigarettes answered, "Hey Harper, how are you? I've been meaning to call..." she trailed off, and although I couldn't see her face, I knew she was face-palming right now.

"Hey, Aunt Linda, I'm doing okay. I'm calling because I was wondering if I could join you all for Christmas this year? Unless you're going on vacation?" I said, a hint of nervousness in my voice.

Without missing a beat, she answered, "We actually aren't going anywhere. I'd love it if you could join us, honey. And Marty too! We got a new puppy, so Marty should have a blast!"

We talked for over an hour, and I was glad that I reached out.

After I finished decorating the rest of the house, I shoved heaps of clothes into my suitcase. I decided to leave tomorrow, not wanting to spend another second in this house.

I woke up bright and early the next morning to Marty's loud barks. The sunrise was peeking through the curtains as I sat up, threw off the covers, and headed into the kitchen. I poured dog food into his bowl and stepped back, watching him devour the food in seconds before spilling his water all over the floor. After that, I took a quick shower and loaded the bags in the car, let Marty out before locking up the house to take off. The car ride was only going to be four hours, but I had never driven it myself before. My mom knew the route by heart, while I had to pull up GPS to figure it out.

After making one stop, I finally arrived at their house a little over four hours later.

My aunt swung open the door before I even stepped foot on the porch and Marty went running into the house to escape the cold snow.

A smile on my face appeared as I walked into my aunt's embrace and looked over her shoulder to see Marty playing with their dog, Sammy.

"How are you doing, sweetheart? I'm so happy you could join us this year!" She looked at me with a warm smile as I took a few steps into the house and out of the cold.

"I'm doing okay, thanks for having me over." I plastered on a smile and glanced around the house. Her house was much more decorated than in previous years, but it felt more jolly in a sense, and I wondered if that was to get her sister's death off her mind. The next day or two was uneventful as I caught up with my aunt over the details of what exactly happened with my mom, which was harder than I was anticipating. We bawled on and off for days, but it felt good to share my grief with someone else, although that might be morbid to say.

I thought things were finally taking a turn and we were getting our minds off my mother until I overheard whispering downstairs in the kitchen. I was on my way to grab a glass of water and stopped midway on the stairs and sat down, wondering what it could be about. Unmistakably, I heard Linda's trembling voice as she talked to her daughter, Cassie.

"I don't understand why Harper didn't say anything to us about Betty's cancer. Why would she hide that? Betty was my sister, for goodness' sake."

They continued whispering for several more minutes, though it was hard to make out due to Marty's snoring a few feet away from me. Still thirsty, I headed back upstairs, not wanting to intrude or get into that conversation tonight.

I could feel the tension in the room as soon as I stepped foot in the kitchen the next day. We'd spent most of the day baking cookies and other desserts, but it was hard to do that with their deafening silence.

While Cassie and Aunt Linda were quiet, Alison didn't seem to have a clue of their conversation the night before. I thought about dropping it, not giving it another thought, but considering the two appeared to be keeping me at arm's length, I wasn't sure how long I could do that.

After about an hour of this awkwardness, I took my aunt aside to talk to her. "I didn't know my mom had cancer until the day she died."

My aunt looked at me in confusion for randomly bringing this up, so I continued, "I overheard you last night talking to Cassie. I just wanted to tell you that I had no clue she was even sick, and I wasn't trying to hide anything from you."

Tears formed in my aunt's eyes at this confession, and she wrapped her arms tightly across her chest as if she was trying to soothe herself. "How could she not say anything? Especially not to you? She loved you more than life itself, she should've fought to save herself."

My aunt was posing questions that had been swirling in my mind ever since I left the hospital, though I'd had a lot more time to think about it than my aunt had.

"I think she knew she wouldn't have beat this, and she didn't want to rack up hundreds of thousands of dollars in bills and put herself through hell just to die anyway. She didn't want me to persuade her into getting treatment because she already made up her mind and she didn't know how to tell me she wasn't going to fight."

My aunt stood there, taking it all in as I rambled. I'm not sure if I needed to hear those words out loud more, or if she did. She wrapped me up in another hug again, and I felt a few tears land on my shoulder as she whispered, "Thank you for telling me this, honey."

Later that night, my aunt, my cousins, and I sat around on the couches, sipping on some hot chocolate.

"Harper, what Christmas traditions did you used to do with your mom?" my aunt asked. She bore a sad smile as she asked this, and I hadn't even thought about it until then.

"We liked to drive around neighborhoods and rank their Christmas lights."

She raised her eyebrows. "Oh, really? That sounds like fun!"

So, after finishing our mugs of hot chocolate, we headed out into the cold and into the car to check out the nearby neighborhoods.

I liked going to different neighborhoods for once, instead of the same ones over and over. We drove around for about an hour until we hit some slick spots on the road. I was thankful they were incorporating some of my traditions with my mom; it meant more to me than they realized, as I was fighting back tears on the drive home.

When Christmas finally rolled around, I wasn't expecting any presents. I had only called to join a few days before, but somehow my name was on a few of the gifts underneath the tree. I smiled at my aunt as I unwrapped them, thanking her for the gift cards and books. When I woke up that morning, I dreaded going downstairs and pretending to be as happy as I would've been with my mom. I'm not saying I wasn't grateful for my aunt letting me come over, but it was just different, and I wasn't sure how long it was going to take to get used to that.

"Wait, Harper, I have one more thing to give you." She rushed upstairs and came back down with a sweater in her hand before handing it to me. "This was your mother's. I'd like you to have it." I thanked her as I tucked it closer to my chest. She glanced around at the presents she gave me and added, "I know it's not much, but I hope you know how much it means to me that you came over for Christmas. And we'd love to keep having you over."

As I stood in the doorway getting ready to leave a few days later, I realized how much I enjoyed spending time there. And it was certainly getting harder to leave, seeing that Marty would not budge from Sammy. For the entire time we were there, Marty was glued to Sammy and acted like an entirely new dog.

"I know this is asking a lot, and you've already done so much for me, but I was wondering if you guys wanted to keep Marty?"

I could tell that Linda loved the idea immediately, but downplayed it. "Oh no, honey. We couldn't take him from you!"

"I'm going back to college in a few months, and I can't bring him to the dorm with me," I said as I looked at Marty who was playing with Sammy with a dog toy.

She glanced over at the two dogs, a smile on her face. "They sure do get along great. Are you sure?"

I nodded, though the tears in my eyes disagreed with me. I knew it was best, but now I truly had to face an empty house. A house without the sound of my mother's voice and Marty's loud barks. I gave my aunt one final hug goodbye, hoping I made the right decision.

A few hours later, I plopped down on the couch, looking at the lively Christmas decorations. I didn't feel much in the Christmas spirit, not that I had in the first place. Despite several hours of being in the car and wanting to melt into the couch, I couldn't. I glanced at the decorations and felt the undeniable urge to take it all down. I put everything in a bin and shoved it into the closet.

The Start of the New Year

My New Years' Eve was nothing exciting; I fell asleep before midnight. I never really liked the holiday, even before this year. I wasn't going to do the whole "new year, new me" bullshit. But I also realized I couldn't be living the way I had been. Since my mother's death, I truly hadn't been out of the house much. I was eating the food my neighbors and friends brought me, and online grocery shopped whenever I ran out, but other than that I mainly ventured from my room to the living room. After my Keurig broke and I was too tired to start my day without coffee, I decided to head to the local Starbucks. As I predicted, it was awfully busy, but I managed to grab the last table. I brought my laptop, though I'm not really sure why, I hadn't opened it for months. I couldn't look into the fall literature and writing classes yet, and I hadn't worked on any of my stories since before my mother's death. If I was going to go back to NYU, I wanted to at least have something written, though I had no idea what. I opened up the laptop and stared at a blank page and blinking cursor for longer than I care to admit. I was on the precipice of typing a word (who am I kidding, no I wasn't) before a throat cleared beside me.

"Do you mind if I sit here with you? There are no more tables and I drove all this way. I'll sit on the far end; you won't even know I'm here." He flashed a smile.

"Yeah, no worries." He set his things down and headed straight to the long line. He sat down with what appeared to be a simple black coffee and a cake pop, which he handed to me.

"Oh, you didn't have to do that," I said, as I took it from his hands.

He shrugged his shoulders and opened his laptop. He then was quiet for a while, but I still felt better with someone sitting next to me, even if we weren't going to talk anymore.

"So, are you in college?" he asked, looking up from his screen. I narrowed my eyes at the random question, before I noticed him eyeing my NYU sweatshirt that I forgot I had on.

"I was enrolled in NYU in the fall, but I'm taking a semester off and starting back in a couple of months."

"Oh really? I go there too!" he said as he closed his laptop, fully knowing he wasn't going to get anything else done.

"Are you taking a semester off, too?" I asked, seeing that it was a random Wednesday.

He shook his head. For a split second, I thought I saw his face drop, but a grin popped through. "Oh no, I just had a family thing I needed to come back for."

We ended up talking for hours, and I broke down and bought one of their little sandwiches to stop the rumbling in my stomach. He left shortly after the midday rush and I sat there for a few minutes, feeling better than I had in months. That was until I stood up. My butt was numb from sitting in the chair too long, but despite the stiff walk back to my car, I didn't regret a second of it.

I felt lighter as I walked into my mom's house. I wish I had done that sooner, not been a recluse in the house and avoided seeing people. While I had kept some contact with my friends and would give the same usual wave or round of small talk with the neighbors, I hadn't really talked to someone in a while. As I sat on the couch, I wondered if he would be there tomorrow. Wouldn't hurt to go back, right?

So, I woke up early the next morning, brought my laptop, and sat down at the same spot as the day before. The Starbucks barista didn't look very lively this morning, as she took my order monotonously. I got my usual this time of year, a peppermint mocha, and opened up my laptop to actually work on something this time. It was hard enough to get into the creative writing program at NYU, and since I had so much free time on my hands, I knew I needed to start writing again. Once I started, I didn't stop typing for about an hour until I heard a chair scrape close to me. I looked up and felt a small smile appear when the guy from yesterday sat down.

"Mind if I join you?"

I shook my head and pushed my things aside.

He sat there for a second, twiddling his thumbs, before he said, "You know, after talking with you yesterday, I realized I never got your name."

I blushed at this for some reason and responded, "Harper."

"Jack." He slumped back in his chair, as though the nervousness he had felt dissipated upon hearing my name. "What are you drinking today?" he asked.

"Peppermint mocha," I replied simply.

He nodded. "I'm gonna give that a try." He ordered his drink, and moments later he sat down again, flipping his laptop open.

"What are you working on today?" I asked, trying to get a sense of why he was here.

"Assignments for my architecture classes before I head back this weekend."

Disappointment ran through me when he said this. After he said he went to NYU, I knew he would have to go back, I just hoped it wouldn't be this soon. He noticed I grew quiet at this and asked what I was up to.

I sat for a second. "I'm writing today."

"May I ask what it's about, or is it too early?" He flashed me a grin and leaned forward on the table.

"It's about my mom. She, um..." I took a big breath before continuing, "She passed away in October."

His eyes widened at this, and he nodded knowingly. I could see tears forming in his eyes as he said, "I'm sorry to hear that. My dad actually passed last week from a car accident."

An awkward silence ensued after that, but I expressed my condolences to him, and he gave me a curt smile. After a few minutes had passed, I struck up another conversation with him which led to us talking as long as we did the day before.

He asked, "I know I'm going back to school in a few days, and I hope I'm not being too forward, but can I have your number?"

As soon as he gave me his number, there wasn't a day that went by when we weren't texting or calling. He was excelling in his classes, while I was trying to figure out how to move on with my life. Living in my mom's house wasn't easy, and I didn't know how much longer I wanted to stay. I knew I probably should sell it by the time I went back to college, but the thought of going through everything was daunting. Jack would come home once a month to see me and check up on his mom and sisters, and it was a long couple of months before he came home for the summer. For me, in those months I hadn't accomplished much. I wrote from time to time, and tried to upkeep the house, but I knew sooner or later that I would have to go through her things and mine. I didn't have the heart to do it until Jack swung by to help.

I stood in the living room for a few minutes after he came over, overwhelmed with how much there was to do.

"What's wrong?" he asked, rubbing my shoulders as tears pricked my eyes.

"It feels wrong to go through her things, because I keep expecting her to walk through the door. But I know I need to." I sighed before I dropped on my knees to the floor and started going through her pile of movies.

Hints

Although I didn't pick up on them then, my mom began dropping hints of her death about six months before she passed. She talked excessively about what to do with the money she saved for my degree, and would talk to me about how to budget my money. I wish she would've used that money for her cancer treatment, but I can't change that now.

There were warning signs that I overlooked. She had rapidly lost weight, but she explained it was a new diet that she started. She always seemed exhausted and frail, but I chalked it up to the beauty of her getting older.

She also worked a lot along with her full-time job. She was either always crafting or sometimes would DoorDash to make money. I didn't understand it, especially with how much money she made from her regular job. But I would help her with crafting creations to sell them on Etsy, or tag along with her on her DoorDash runs. What I didn't realize then was why she was trying to make as much money as she possibly could. She told me it was so we could go on a longer trip before I headed off to college, but now thinking about it, I knew it was because this would be her last trip she'd ever take.

We'd go on one trip, maybe two, each year. Normally, we would pile ourselves into the car and would drive to a nearby state and check out a national park or whatever we wanted, really. But when I was 15, we started visiting states with big colleges to help with my decision of where to go. Truthfully, I wanted to go to a local college in Colorado to not be far from my mom. However, my mother insisted on going to colleges like the University of Chicago or Indiana University, but in particular, New York University. As soon as I stepped foot onto NYU's campus, it felt like home. I downplayed that, of course; I didn't want my mom to know how much I loved it.

"If you don't go here, I'm going to be pissed at you," my mom said when we sat down in the car. My mom had also gone to NYU, and she said it was some of the best years of her life. She lived in New York until she was pregnant with me, but she only moved because she wanted to escape city life and live in the mountains. And that's what she did. While we were in New York, we visited all of her favorite places.

When I found out I was accepted, I don't think I've ever seen her more excited. She cried happy tears for over an hour, and then decided that we wanted to make the most of our last summer together. That's when she decided to work extra to save up for that trip. During that summer, we visited the remaining national parks that we hadn't seen yet before hitting a few beaches.

I didn't want the trip to end, but summer went by quickly, and before I knew it, we were standing in my new dorm room. As I imagined, it was tiny, but there was still enough room to decorate and fit all of what I brought.

I guess another hint I should've picked up on was how winded she got when we moved my things in. Granted we had to make a few trips and climb some stairs, but it seemed to completely wipe her out. After the third trip, she resorted to lying on the bed while I hauled the rest in, not that I minded. She actually fell asleep and slept for a good thirty minutes while I began hanging my clothes in the sorry excuse for a closet. When she woke up, she glanced around the room, before her eyes landed on me and she apologized and attributed it to the long drive that we had. I brushed it off and believed her.

A few hours later, as she was leaving to head back to Colorado, she had tears in her eyes, though I expected her to. But what I didn't expect her to say was, "You'll be just fine without me, okay?"

. . .

Advice

I now know in the end she wanted to protect me, not paralyze me with fear or anticipatory grief. She knew I wouldn't have gone to college had I known about the cancer. My mom was known to be an advice-giver, whether you wanted it or not.

She chalked it up to being 45 years old when she had me, and said there was no sense in beating around the bush. She told everything to me straight, especially if I didn't want to hear it. She said something inspirational from time to time, but in the year before I left for college, especially during that summer, she'd have a new piece of advice every day--though most of those originated from a calendar that she bought that gave positive sayings. She'd read it herself first, and then she'd plop it next to my breakfast plate to start my day.

She was extroverted and could talk to anyone with no hesitation, even if it was someone she met in a line in the McDonald's lobby. I, however, wasn't. On the way to college, my mom said, "I want you to get out there and meet people, okay? Don't rot away in your dorm room, don't be afraid to talk to people. Be yourself. There's nothing wrong with just starting a conversation."

And I did that with my roommate and friends in college, and with Jack. There was never any advice that I wouldn't take, because she always led and pushed me in the right direction. She'd push me to go to homecoming or football games instead of just staying in all the time; she'd tell me to try out a new hobby or restaurant; she was my sounding board for everything. But the only thing she didn't give me advice on was how to cope with her death and live a life without her.

Packing Things Away

I found out early on in the packing process that I would need to rent a storage locker. I had a hard time letting things go, despite knowing that I couldn't keep everything. It practically took me all summer to go through everything and make decisions, and I ended up sending several boxes of things over to my aunt.

The end of summer came up faster than I was anticipating, and Jack and I drove my car up to college, seeing that I had to move back into the dorm room. Within the last week, I sold my mother's house, which was relieving and devastating at the same time. As much as I hated it, I knew it was time. NYU was waiting for me, and I hoped I would still feel as close to my mom in New York as I did in her house. I mainly took her clothes and some of her furniture for my next place, and on the day the house sold, I stood outside staring at it for well over an hour. It was the only house I've ever lived in, and I hoped my mom would understand why I had to sell it.

The Dreaded Anniversaries

Every year, no matter what I have going on, I never seem to be able to get out of bed on the anniversary of her death. Flashbacks of her laying in the hospital bed. with what seemed to be a thousand needles and tubes poking out of her, popped up in my mind each morning on the anniversary.

The first year, Jack let me wallow in bed. He brought me snacks and drinks and watched movies with me until the sun went down. I was a blubbering mess most of the day, but I couldn't have made it through that day without him.

I had planned on doing the same thing the next year, but Jack had other ideas. He threw open the curtains, the light burning my eyes as I shimmied underneath the blankets, which he promptly took off seconds later. He stared down at me, his eyes full of concern, as he said, "Your mom wouldn't want you to wallow like this, okay? Let's go do something and get your mind off her."

I groaned, and he smiled. He leaned down and picked me up, knowing I wouldn't get up unless he made me.

"Alright, now I've got some things planned and you're following along, okay?"

I nodded, a small smile on my lips as I wondered what the day had in store. The first stop was a bookstore that I had been wanting to visit for years, but never got around to. The next was a local art fair, one that I had attended with my mom numerous times. Before that we ate lunch at one of her favorite restaurants, one that I hadn't stepped foot in since her death. The owner, Lorie, was one of my mom's best friends, and her eyes glossed over at the sight of me.

"Hey, Harper. It's been a while... how have you been?"

I blew out a breath, and she followed with, "I know, a silly question with how everything happened, but I've thought about you every day since she passed."

"Thanks, Lorie. I've actually been doing okay, but I still have moments where I forget she's gone." She nodded in agreement. "I don't know where I'd be if I didn't have my boyfriend, Jack." Jack smiled and introduced himself to Lorie.

"Well, don't be a stranger, okay?" she said. "I'm here for you."

I thanked her and we ate our lunch, and I couldn't get out of the restaurant fast enough.

I slammed the car door, leaning my head on the headrest as I tried to will away the threatening tears, but failed. By the time Jack got in, I had a steady stream of tears down my cheeks, sobs breaking through as he reached over and grabbed my hand, rubbing it gently as I slowly calmed down.

"Was this too much?" Jack asked, his voice barely above a whisper.

I shook my head. "No, I needed to do this. I can't keep avoiding anything that reminds me of her anymore."

We spent the rest of the afternoon cuddling on the couch, and Mom remained on my mind, as she always did, for the entire night.

The next year, he proposed at her gravesite. While that might sound morbid to most, it felt like she was there with me, and I couldn't have asked for a more perfect moment.

The House

My mom and I had a grand plan of what our dream house would look like. This plan started when I was six, and kept going until I was a few months away from high school. My mom drew up plans for the layout, and even included details down to the paint color, and although I knew we probably would never move into a house like this, I liked seeing how excited she was every time she rolled out the plans.

It wasn't that we didn't like the house we lived in, but my mom dreamed of a house that she could fully design herself, down to the structure.

I forgot about the plans until I pulled the papers out of the drawer of her bedside table that I kept, along with some of her other furniture. I showed Jack, and he indulged in my long-winded explanation behind every decision my mom and I made, before I set it in our bottom desk drawer in our starter home.

It had been about seven years since my mom's death at that point. I kept some of her furniture, and set it around our house in an effort to keep her close to me. I still thought about her every day, though as much as I hated it, it was getting easier to live without her.

About a year and a half after showing Jack those house plans, Jack told me that he had been working on building us a house. I forgot that I had showed him those plans, as I had pregnancy brain now that I was pregnant with our first child, a girl. She was coincidentally due on the same day my mother died. As much as I didn't want to give birth on that day, I was hoping she would be born on her due date. I still had trouble getting through that day, and the thought of my daughter sharing that day would give it new meaning.

Jack told me he was going to build a house for us, but I didn't believe him. He worked more than the average person, but I guess I didn't account that those late nights meant he was working on the house.

About two months before our daughter was born, Jack and I had packed all of our belongings and were heading over to the new house, which I was anxious to see. He hadn't shown me any of the plans the entire time he was building, but when we pulled into the driveway, tears streamed down my face immediately.

The house had every single design element that my mother thought of, and I couldn't have been more in awe. Any time I walked around in the house, I thought of my mom and how much she would've loved it. It hasn't been easy without her, but I wouldn't be where I am without her. I wouldn't have met Jack and I wouldn't have had my daughter, Maeve Betty Johnson.

The best thing of all? She was born on her due date.

CHAPTER 15

The Ranking

The Ranking:
Roman
Willa
Hadley
Beau
Kieran
Lottie

Lottie

Paige didn't tell her friends why she put their names in a list. Or what it meant. When Lottie saw the notebook flipped to the page, a million thoughts ran through her head. She stared at it for a few minutes before asking, "What is this?"

Lottie had always felt somewhat like an outsider to the group, so when she saw her name last, her mind immediately switched to that. Paige stayed silent, which annoyed Lottie.

"Dude," Lottie said. "Seriously, what is this?"

Paige shrugged her shoulder and Lottie, not wanting to make a big deal over what could be nothing, decided to head outside and escape it.

They were on a cabin trip, a relaxing vacation for everyone to take their minds off work and "enjoy nature." Paige had a high-paying job, something she liked to brag about often, and decided to pay for everyone. But along with that came some rules:

1) No phones or any devices
2) No TV, spend as much time outside as possible
3) Have fun

Lottie attempted to follow the last two rules by laying outside on a flimsy beach towel, trying to soak up the sun. As for rule three, she found that to be hard, seeing as she couldn't stop thinking about the list of their names. Lottie knew Paige prided herself on being a cryptic person. For what reason Lottie didn't know, but she knew that it was her least favorite thing about Paige. In fact, Lottie couldn't even tell you what Paige did for work, She just knew it paid well, and the size of the cabin was proof. When Lottie pulled up in her car, her eyes widened and her jaw dropped. When she stepped inside, she noticed that despite there being seven people on this trip, there were only six bedrooms. This wasn't important, since they could share beds, and Lottie appreciated the decked-out cabin, nonetheless.

Lottie spent over a half hour examining every square inch of that cabin. There was no doubt it had been completely renovated, with its quartz countertops, top-of-the-line appliances, and hardwood floors. Lottie would gladly live here if she could. It certainly beat the place she already lived in-- thin-as-a-sheet walls, two roommates who were about as inconsiderate as they come--but she couldn't afford the place by herself, so she dealt with it.

When Paige invited her to go on this trip she agreed in a heartbeat, needing a break from her irritating roommates. The trip had barely started, and she was enjoying herself more in the last few minutes than she had in the past several months.

That was, until she saw that list.

Lottie knew that she shouldn't let it get to her; she couldn't recall the last time she had been on a vacation. But it lingered in the back of her mind.

As she felt her skin tighten from the overwhelmingly hot sun, her mind kept raking through the possibilities of what the list meant.

Could it be that I was the last one to be invited? she thought to herself. It couldn't be that easy, right?

She sat up, wiping the thin line of sweat from her forehead, and moved to the shade. She didn't want to get a sunburn already when it hadn't even been two hours since she got here. And while it probably wasn't good to be alone with her thoughts and the mystery behind that list, this was the most peaceful she had felt in a long time. She wasn't much of a nature lover before this, but hearing the waves of the lake, she could see now why others found it appealing.

A few minutes later, Paige sat down next to her. She still sported the same smirk she had worn earlier, and it took all that was in Lottie not to roll her eyes at this. Lottie often debated whether or not she wanted to be friends with Paige. There were times when Paige acted like the best friend you could ever have, showering you with gifts, or just being there for you when you needed it. And then, other times, you wouldn't want to get closer than ten feet to her, her malicious side coming into play. You didn't want to get on her bad side.

But truthfully, Paige was the glue that held this friend group together. Lottie liked everyone else, but she noticed they didn't all hang out together if Paige wasn't there. So, Lottie put up with Paige's antics, but she wondered how far this one would go. Most of the time Lottie could put the antics aside, but not this time, especially because of that stupid little smirk.

Lottie was seconds away from confronting Paige when the sliding door opened, and Beau stepped out. He had sunglasses on, but as soon as he felt the tension coming from Lottie and Paige, he took them off, showcasing his beautiful ocean-blue eyes. He glanced between the two of them, not saying anything for a minute, before he finally said, "What the fuck did I just walk out to? You two already fighting or something?"

Lottie glanced over at Paige and raised her eyebrows, cueing Paige to spill. Instead, Paige kept quiet and shook her head, which resulted in an eye roll and an over-exasperated sigh from Lottie.

"Alright, fine. Paige has a list of our names written in a list in her notebook and she won't tell me what it's for."

Beau

As soon as Lottie said that, Beau shot daggers at Paige.

Of course, she would fucking pull a stunt like this.

Beau knew she most likely set that list out for Lottie to discover, knowing it would eat her alive for the entire trip. Shit like this was why Beau broke up with Paige last year. Granted, they only dated for a couple of months, but Beau couldn't stand her little mind games. He was half surprised that Paige had invited him here in the first place, as she wasn't happy with the breakup. She called Beau several times a day for two weeks until she got the hint. She had moved on to some other guy quickly while Beau vowed to stay single for a while, needing a mental reset. It was hostile for a bit, until Paige called a truce when she met Roman. After that, she became cordial with Beau, and he was officially back in the friend group.

When Beau first met Roman, he thought he was kind, perhaps even a little too kind for Paige. It had been a little over six months since they started dating, and he didn't know how Roman could still put up with her. Beau hoped Roman would make Paige change her ways, but hearing about this stupid little list, Beau knew that wasn't the case.

"This better not be one of your stupid little games, Paige," he said.

"It's not," Paige replied, though Beau knew it was far from the truth.

"Lottie," Beau said, and she perked up, staring at him. "Can you show me which room you want? I don't want to steal it."

She stood up immediately, a relieved look on her face as she passed by Paige and into the house. He made sure the door was closed, and was tempted to lock it to keep Paige outside, but decided against it.

"I wanted the room with the view of the lake," Lottie said, walking to show him which one, but he grabbed her arm, stopping her.

"I saw your stuff in there," he said. "I really just wanted you to show me that list."

She nodded, and directed him to the dining room table. Paige must've closed the book, because Lottie flipped it open to the first page where their names were scribbled in.

Beau crouched down and skimmed the names, as dumbfounded over their meaning as Lottie was. It piqued his curiosity too, but he couldn't let Lottie know that, because she'd be obsessing about it over the next four days, and Lord knows she didn't need that. Beau had always had a soft spot for Lottie; probably because he'd had a crush on her for who knows how long. But he always assumed she wouldn't feel the same, therefore he settled on Paige. He knew now that had been a mistake.

"Do you have any ideas?" Lottie asked.

Beau ran his fingers on the paper and shook his head. "None," he mumbled, his eyes glued to the paper, before Kieran walked in.

Kieran

Kieran had already finished a beer and was throwing it away when Beau motioned him over to the table. "What?" Kieran asked.

"Come take a look at this and tell us what you think," Beau said.

Kieran walked over and scanned the paper, taking in the names.

"What the hell is this?" Kieran asked, before adding, "Damn, I'm near the bottom with you, Lottie." He laughed before heading towards the fridge and grabbing another beer, popping it open, and taking a large swig.

"Does it bother you?" Lottie asked.

"Not particularly, don't even know what it means." He burped. "Let me take a guess: this was the workings of Paige."

Beau nodded, and Kieran shrugged it off.

"Listen, I don't give a fuck about whatever Paige meant by this. I'm not falling for her shit. I say we forget about it and just have fun."

With Kieran's suggestion, and his forking over two beers to them, Lottie and Beau let loose and forgot about the list.

They were about four or five beers in when Willa and Hadley finally arrived after not being able to take the day off work. Smiles perked on their faces immediately as they took in the sight of Kieran, who was more than a little tipsy.

"Hey! You guys made it!" he slurred. He ran over to the fridge and handed beers to Willa and Hadley, and they all drank the rest of the night...except for one.

Paige stayed outside most of the night before coming in. She brushed past everyone, and headed to bed.

Hadley

Hadley had dreaded coming to this cabin. She was surprised she was even invited, considering she had fallen out with Paige not even two weeks before. Hadley was usually the first to apologize, but she refused to this time.

It was a stupid fight really. Hadley asked to borrow some outfits for interviews, and Paige threw a hissy at her for even asking. Apparently, Hadley had ruined a shirt of hers in the past, so Paige made it this whole big thing.

But then, Paige went and invited Hadley to the cabin anyway, so Hadley rolled with it.

When Paige stormed through the living room later that night, her usual resting bitch face on display, Hadley thought Paige was still harboring ill-will for her. But after Paige slammed the door, she quickly learned that wasn't the case.

Lottie, who was nursing her sixth beer, not so quietly asked, "Did you take a look at that fucking notebook yet?"

Hadley narrowed her eyes at this, not having any indication of what she meant. Beau rubbed his forehead, and Hadley guessed it was either because they'd talked about this already, or because he, too, was hammered.

He motioned for her to be quiet, and she nodded, before he said, "Paige wrote our names in a list in her notebook and won't tell us what it means."

Hadley looked at Willa, who bore an annoyed expression on her face.

"Why would she do that?"

"Hell if I know," Beau said.

Hadley stood up, walked towards the notebook, and grabbed it before returning to her spot on the loveseat. Her name was third on the list, and she showed Willa that hers was second. Hadley closed the book and set it on the side table.

"Roman, you got any idea?"

He shook his head. "None."

Hadley knew Roman hated fighting with Paige, mainly because he could never get a word in. But that's how most arguments would go with Paige. Even if she was fighting multiple people at once, she always somehow found a way to win.

"Well," Hadley said, "has anyone confronted her about this?"

Lottie answered with, "I tried asking, but you know how she is."

Hadley nodded knowingly and said, "Why don't we just forget about it for now, okay? We're on vacation, so let's not make this stupid little list ruin it. Don't even bring it up to Paige anymore. Let's forget and have fun."

Everyone agreed, and headed to bed soon afterwards, knowing they'd all have hangovers in the morning.

Willa

The first thought that popped into Willa's mind a few hours later was, *Who is making breakfast?*

Willa chugged the water she set on the nightstand; she was happy she hadn't had as much to drink as everyone else. She still had a small headache, but at least it wasn't a splitting one. She threw her robe and slippers on before making her way to the kitchen. Paige stood there with a bunch of food made.

"Morning," said Paige. "Made some muffins if you wanna grab one."

"That sounds perfect. Thanks, Paige."

Willa took a big bite, expecting to taste blueberries or chocolate chips, but didn't taste either. She swallowed the bite and inspected the muffin, which had speckles of yellow within it. "Paige, what kind of muffin is this?"

Without turning around, Paige replied, "It's an egg muffin. There are some vegetables in it, and eggs, obviously."

"Why didn't you tell me that before I took a bite?" Willa replied, throwing the muffin down in a panic.

"They're just breakfast muffins, what's the big deal?" Paige turned around, a hand on her hip as she stared at Willa with a frown.

"I'm allergic to eggs, you know that!" Willa's voice was raised.

"You've made eggless muffins for me before, you've always made sure to not bake muffins with eggs."

Heavy footsteps rang down the hallway before Beau appeared, looking rough as well. He had one sock on, and his pants were riding dangerously low. Beau stood next to Willa, smelling of beer that seeped from his pores. He glanced at the stalemate stare between the two women. "Catfight already?"

"If you wanna call it that." Willa coughed, her throat already sounding wheezy.

"You okay?" Beau took a step back from her.

Willa had sweat beading on her top lip and her face looked dangerously pale.

"Those muffins had eggs, Beau. I took a bite."

Beau's eyebrows raised.

"Shit, where's your EpiPen?" Beau asked. Willa pointed to her purse, and Beau sifted through it quickly, coming up with nothing. "Did you not bring one, Willa?"

"There's not one in my purse?" Willa slurred, the swelling already starting.

"No, there's not," Beau replied. His anger visibly grew as Paige stood there, motionless.

"Are you just going to stand there, Paige?" Beau yelled.

"What am I going to be able to do? Just go take her to an Urgent Care or something."

Beau sighed and picked up Willa, who began growing delirious, and ran her to the car. “Thanks a lot, Paige.”

Lottie

The sound of buzzing filled Lottie’s ears, and she jerked awake in a second. Her eyes were still closed, her body stiff, as fear multiplied within her.

Hesitantly, she opened her eyes, screaming as she saw dozens of crickets in her bed and scattered along the floor. Almost slipping, she jumped around the crickets, trying to get out of the bug-infested room. She ran into the hallway outside her room where Kieran stood.

“Why the hell are you screaming?” Kieran asked, his hands covering his ears.

“There’s a swarm of crickets in my room,” Lottie said, out of breath. “There’s no bugs in your room?” Kieran shook his head.

Paige walked by, her face downcast, though Lottie swore she saw her smile.

“Paige?” Lottie said.

“Hmm?” Paige’s eyebrows raised. That half-smirk still remained on her face, and Lottie wanted nothing more than to slap it away.

“In reserving this cabin, were there any mentions of bugs or anything like that?”

“No, there weren’t any negative reviews of bugs. Maybe you were just unlucky. Just get a broom and pan and sweep them out. You’re making this a bigger deal than it is,” Paige said, before walking away.

Lottie had half a mind to yell at Paige, but she swallowed the urge. "Where are Willa and Beau?"

Kieran filled her in on Willa's allergic reaction.

"I'm sick of this shit," Lottie said. "Unlucky my ass."

Hadley

"You sure you wanna do that?" Lottie asked, a hint of fear on her face upon looking at Hadley's laptop.

"Do what?" Hadley replied, her hands moving fast across the keyboard.

"You know, be on a device. It was one of Paige's rules. She's been weird on this trip, I'd just put it away," Lottie answered.

"I'm not gonna let her dictate what I do on this trip. It's my vacation, too. I'm on a deadline for this book and I won't be able to relax until I catch up some."

As if on cue, Paige strolled into the kitchen, her face screwed into a scowl when she saw the laptop.

"I said no electronics, remember," Paige said, shooting daggers at Hadley, who shook it off.

"I'll be done in a few minutes, I just need to finish this one scene, Paige. It's not a big deal." The clacking of her laptop keys seemed to echo in the tense, silent room. Paige sported an annoyed look on her face at Hadley's "defiance" before she headed to the kitchen sink to fill a cup of water. Paige took a tiny sip, then strode up behind Hadley, dumping the entire cup of water on the laptop.

Hadley lifted the laptop, water dripping onto the floor as she screamed. "What the fuck, Paige? I hadn't backed anything up! Why the hell would you do that?"

"Maybe you'll listen to me next time when I tell you to do something," Paige answered, a smirk on her smug face.

Hadley threw the laptop on the counter in a huff. She raised her hand, a mere few inches from Paige, before Kieran rushed up and held her back.

"Don't," he said. "She's not worth it."

Hadley's eyes glistened with tears, while Kieran grabbed a towel and dabbed her laptop dry. He took Hadley into the bedroom and attempted to see what could be revived from her damp computer. Her cries could be heard from the closed door, while Paige sat on the couch without a care in the world.

~~ Later, Paige left to go on a walk, while the rest of the group stayed behind.

Willa and Beau returned from Urgent Care, though Willa curled up on the couch seconds after stepping through the door; the events of the morning had worn her out. Beau sat down in the chair adjacent to her, stress lining his tired face.

Lottie stood behind the couch where Willa lay, petting her hair, as her gentle snores filled the room.

"Is she okay?" she asked Beau, who nodded slightly.

"Yeah, she's fine now. Barely made it in time though. Her throat closed up fast. She might be out of it for the rest of the day." Beau rubbed his hand over his face in an attempt to expel some of the stress coursing through his body. "Fucking Paige and those muffins."

He glanced around the room, hoping Roman didn't hear that, before adding, "Where the hell is Roman?"

Roman

Roman somehow found himself sleeping outside all night, despite his incessant pounding on all the windows and doors. Well, sleeping was generous to say; he spent most of the night listening to the creatures in the nearby woods. If he had to guess, he must've passed out two hours before.

Muffled voices in the living room woke him up, and his head pounded as he slowly got to his feet. Every bone and joint in his body ached.

He knocked on the door, thankful to see his friends in the living room. Lottie's jaw hung open upon seeing his disheveled state before she rushed to open the door.

"What the hell are you doing out here? Did you *sleep* out here?"

"I didn't try to," he said. "I probably banged on the windows and doors a few hundred times." Roman's eyes were brimmed red and he didn't look like he had slept a wink.

Lottie grabbed a blanket and threw it over him; her fingers touched his cold skin and she gasped. "Here, let's get you warmed up."

She led Roman to the open couch, and he lay down, shivering as he tried to warm his freezing body up. She brewed a cup of coffee, hoping the warm liquid would provide some relief.

Lottie saw his handprints scattered along the windows and winced. She handed Roman the cup, and he downed the coffee in a few minutes.

"I'm sorry about last night, Roman," Lottie said, rubbing her hand on his arm.

"So no one heard me?" Roman asked in a small voice.

"I took a sleeping pill last night, I was out cold. Maybe the windows are soundproof?" Lottie offered, and he shrugged his shoulders. The chattering of Roman's teeth had subsided, though he still appeared to be chilled to the bone, and frankly upset.

"You warmed up now, Roman?" Kieran asked.

"Somewhat," Roman replied, although he could've spent the rest of the trip indoors after what he had endured the night before.

"Alright, let's go back outside." Kieran clapped, attempting to rouse excitement, though it fell flat. "Let's refocus on the lake and get away from this house."

"I don't know, man, I--" Roman started, but Kieran interrupted.

"Just for a little while, Roman. It might be relaxing to be out on the water. No offense, but you look like hell." Kieran jutted his bottom lip out and Roman sighed.

"Fine, just for a little bit."

Kieran cheered, and Lottie and Roman followed his lead outside. Beau and Willa remained on the couch, not the slightest bit interested in joining them.

The three of them crammed into the canoes sitting on the edge of the lake. Roman looked as though he'd rather be anywhere but on the water, but after more than a couple of splashes from Kieran's paddle, he loosened up. Lottie laughed as the two boys splashed each other, before all their smiles fell.

"Roman?" Kieran started, a nervous look passing over his damp face.

"Yeah?" Roman held the paddle in his lap; the choppy water had calmed down.

"I watched Paige lock the doors last night. Granted, I didn't know you were out there, and maybe she didn't either, but I wanted to see what you've thought of her this trip."

"What do you mean?" Roman's eyebrows raised.

"Well, first she starts it with that damn list, then makes those egg muffins, and ruins Hadley's laptop. I feel like she's intentionally screwing things up, trying to piss people off. I know she's your girlfriend, but damn, she's ruining this trip."

Roman sighed. "I'll talk to her and see what's going on."

Kieran nodded with a grin which quickly turned into a shriek as he noticed a hole in the canoe, filling with water. "What the hell? There's a damn hole on this canoe!"

"Just scoop it out, Kieran. We can head back to the shore now, it's not that big of a deal."

"I can't swim very well, and this water is freezing!" Kieran huffed as he scooped handfuls of water out of his canoe.

"Then why did you suggest going out on the lake?" Roman yelled.

"I didn't anticipate a hole in the damn boat! I thought it would be relaxing, but clearly I was wrong!" Kieran screamed.

By the time the trio reached land, most of Kieran's canoe was underwater. His clothes were soaked as he trotted back to the cabin. "How much do you want to bet that Paige put a hole in this canoe?" Kieran joked, but Roman looked less than enthused.

"Now don't go blaming everything wrong on her. These canoes are old, I'm sure there was a hole in it before we got here, and you just didn't notice."

Kieran threw his hands up in surrender. "Okay, okay. I'm sure you're right. But I'm keeping a close eye on her."

Roman didn't respond, but he couldn't help but wonder if these coincidences were actual coincidences. Now that Roman heard Kieran's reasonings, he needed to get to the bottom of this.

By the time Kieran changed into dry clothes, Paige had returned from her walk. Her face was set deep in a scowl as she headed to her room without a word.

"What's wrong with her?" Hadley asked, and Roman shrugged.

"Have no fucking clue." He followed Paige into the room, and placed his hands on her shoulders lovingly, though she stared straight ahead with disgust. "What's wrong?"

"Nothing," she grumbled.

"Don't give me that, you've been strange this whole trip," Roman replied.

Paige put her hand on her hip, an act she only did when she was upset.

"Fine. I wanted everyone to do a hike together, but then stupid

Willa got an allergic reaction and then when I came back, you were gone."

"You gave Willa that allergic reaction. You've never forgotten about her allergies before, why did you this time?"

"I don't know, I was too busy making breakfast for everyone and it slipped my mind." She sighed. "Where were you this morning?"

"Per Kieran's request I was out on the lake because he said I needed to relax." Paige's eyebrows raised, and Roman added, "Because I spent the night outside last night. I was locked out."

"You were?"

"Yeah, Kieran said you locked the doors. You didn't think to look for me when I didn't come to bed?"

"I was so tired, I thought you climbed in after me and got up before me."

"Well, I didn't..." Roman replied, though she didn't seem too fazed by his previous night's endeavors. "Anyway, let's catch some sun and drink some more. I feel like this trip has derailed a bit."

Paige agreed, but she did isolate herself from everyone as the day went on. Roman tried to include her when he could, but she showed no interest in it. While everyone else was down by the lake fishing on a little dock, Roman separated to find Paige sunbathing by herself. By the look of her reddening skin, she could use some shade, but Paige wasn't someone who liked being told what to do. He sat beside her, sweat beads running down his forehead. Annoyed that he felt the need to ask her again, he plopped down harshly beside her.

"Can you just tell me what's wrong?" he asked, tired of her stand-offish behavior.

"Nothing's wrong," she replied, not looking at him.

"Okay, then why are you acting like this?"

He heard her sigh, and he knew she was growing angry with him.

"Like what, Roman? I'm just trying to relax and get a tan."

"No, you've been isolating yourself from everyone, even though you planned the trip, and frankly you're being a bitch." She narrowed her eyes at that comment. Roman asked, "And why would you even make a list like that, huh?"

"Why does it bother you? Are you curious about what it means?"

"Everybody is, Paige. I don't understand why you'd pull something like this on what's supposed to be a relaxing trip. People already feel like they have to walk on eggshells around you, and then you pull this stunt."

Paige didn't reply, and for the first time, Roman thought he had stumped her in an argument. He felt some pride at this, although he knew he shouldn't.

She turned over, not wanting to look at him, and he took that as a sign to leave her alone. He went down and joined everyone else. He grabbed a fishing rod and cast a line, when Beau came up and stood next to him.

"In the doghouse?" Beau asked, and Roman nodded.

"I have a feeling she's trying to make us miserable this trip with that fucking list."

Lottie

Lottie heard Roman and Beau from a few feet over. She wasn't planning on eavesdropping, but when she saw Roman's disgruntled face after returning from visiting Paige, she couldn't help but be curious. Their conversation mainly started with a heated whispering, before Roman's voice gradually grew louder.

She heard the end of their conversation clearly: "I'm so sick of her shit, man. I'm not sure how much longer I can keep this up." Roman paused for a second. "This damn list has been driving me nuts, dude."

Roman then walked over to the rest of the group and asked, "Does anybody have a clue about what that fucking list means? I'm tired of thinking about it, so it would be great if one of you guys had an idea."

Lottie glanced over at everyone else, but they all shrugged and didn't provide an explanation. Roman blew out an exasperated breath, before Lottie spoke up. "It could be who she likes most to least?"

Roman whipped his head over to her, his eyebrow raised at the suggestion.

He then shook his head and replied, "I'm not sure that's it. I'm definitely not her favorite person after that argument we just had."

"Well, does anyone else have any idea?" Lottie asked, moving some strands of hair out of her face from the blowing wind.

"Maybe it's a list of who was invited, first to last?" Hadley posed, though obviously no one knew if that was the case. Lottie decided that this made sense. It would explain why she was last and why Paige's boyfriend was first. Nobody ventured another guess, and Lottie wished someone had. Now that she knew this list bothered Roman as much as it did her, she wanted to get to the bottom of it.

The group dispersed as soon as a sunburnt Paige walked up.

At this point, to distract himself, Roman kept his eyes on the water, and Lottie had a feeling he hoped he could catch a fish this instant. Paige tried to wrap her arms around his shoulders, but he flinched.

He tried to play it off that she had cold hands, but Lottie knew with that sunburnt skin, she had to be radiating heat. Paige left a few seconds after, presumably feeling the tension from everyone, but that was just a façade. Lottie was sure of it. Her little games were working, and Lottie pictured a smirk on Paige's face as she sauntered away.

Lottie ended up following Paige back to the house, not because she wanted to talk to her, but she was sick of waiting for one of the boys to catch a fish. It had been going on for two hours now, without a single nibble. Her patience had worn thin, but it already had been thin from yesterday. It took all that was in her not to lash out. Paige went inside, while Lottie hung around the back porch. Eventually, one by one, everyone joined Lottie on the porch, and she assumed that they didn't go inside for the same reason she hadn't.

It was growing darker outside, and Lottie's stomach growled. She suggested ordering a few pizzas to keep it simple. Kieran started ordering them through the app, when Lottie asked, "Shouldn't we see what Paige wants?"

Blank faces all around, no one offering a comment, before Willa piped up.

"Why should we? All she's done is isolate herself and be rude this entire trip."

Lottie sighed. "I know, but is this how we wanna spend the rest of this trip?"

Willa mulled this over for a second, then said, "Why don't we beat her at her own game? Let's start by ordering a pizza with mushrooms."

"Mushrooms? But Paige is allergic," Roman said.

"Exactly." Willa smiled. Then she ordered two large mushroom pizzas.

Beau

The shit-eating grin Willa had on her face when she opened the pizza boxes to show Paige was something that Beau would never forget. Paige looked excited to eat the pizza, and pleased that her friends weren't avoiding her for once, but she scowled as she stared at the heaping pile of mushrooms. "You got two mushroom pizzas? I'm allergic."

"Oh really? Didn't know." Willa smiled as she took a bite.

Paige rolled her eyes and pulled out the loaf of bread from the pantry before heading to the fridge to grab some ham. She sat back at the counter and ate her sandwich quietly while everyone else devoured the pizza.

Then, the alcohol followed. Beau promised himself that he wouldn't drink as much, seeing that he just got rid of his headache, but once Lottie started pouring shots, it was game over.

Lottie had brought a few drinking games for the trip. One was called *Buzzed Tower,* where you pick a card and then add blocks to the stack. Beau wasn't much in favor of drinking games, but he liked this one. He admittedly wasn't very good at it, seeing that he knocked over the stack more than a couple of times. Paige ended up playing too, though in their short relationship together he knew that she hated drinking games more than him.

Beau assumed the only reason she joined in was because her little plan backfired. Paige always was a drama-stirrer, and would often take things further than she needed to, a prime example being this list. Beau eyed Paige, but she was looking at Roman. Beau wanted to get to the bottom of this, he didn't want to admit that he still itched to know what that list meant, but he knew that's what Paige does. She gets under your skin and never leaves. In instances like this, Beau wondered why anyone in this room considered Paige a friend.

When he and Paige broke up, all he wanted was for them to be friends. But now, staring at her, he couldn't think of a single reason why he wanted that. Well, other than being able to see Lottie, but apart from that, she brought no value to his life. All he could think about was learning the meaning behind the list, not for himself, but for Lottie. He could tell that while she was enjoying the game, the list still weighed in her mind.

So, before his brain could tell him to stop, he found himself asking Paige to join him in another room to talk. He shut the door behind her, and was moments away from sitting on the bed, when he felt Paige's hands wrap around his neck, pulling his face down to meet her lips. She sloppily kissed him, tasting of sangria, before he stumbled away from her.

"What the fuck was that?" he panted.

She bore a lazy smile as she sat down on the bed.

"Don't act all innocent here, Beau. I've felt you staring at me all night."

Beau's hands reached up in his hair, trying not to explode on her and cause a scene. He thought back, and he knew he hadn't been giving her mixed signals.

"What about Roman?" he asked.

She shrugged. "He was just a distraction to get my mind off of you."

Beau paced around her, hoping that if he kept moving, she wouldn't try to kiss him again. He didn't want to go down that road, getting sucked into her once more. And he didn't want to betray Roman like this, even if Roman seemed to be over Paige's antics, too.

Beau glanced over at Paige. She was sprawled out on the bed.

"I didn't bring you in here to do this," Beau said flatly, not caring if that caused her any embarrassment. Which it did, as her cheeks flared red and she got off the bed immediately.

"Then why did you ask me in here?"

"The list."

She rolled her eyes at this. "Are we still on that, Beau?"

"Don't act like you're annoyed, it's not a good look on you," Beau seethed. "And neither is this feigned indifference over the list. I'm sick of you dictating, having this weird power over this group. You're no better than the rest of us, and the fact that you made this ominous list without telling us what it meant is low, even for you."

Admittedly, he felt lighter after getting that off his chest.

"Tell me how you really feel," she replied, seemingly not absorbing anything he said.

Beau scoffed, fighting the urge to cave in and yell, because he knew that's exactly what she wanted him to do. He exhaled slowly, pinching the bridge of his nose in an attempt to ignore the red-hot anger pooling inside him, begging to be released.

"You're impossible. You know that, right?"

A knowing smirk appeared on her face, and any embarrassment she harbored vanished. Instead, she clearly relished in this feeling she could feel radiating off of him. She liked that she could still rile him up.

"You're really not going to tell us, are you?" Beau sighed, running his hand through his slightly greasy hair. He had been sweating outside, and now he was sweating simply from sharing the same space as Paige.

She shook her head, staying silent, knowing that infuriated him more.

Beau turned towards the door, his knuckles white from gripping the door handle entirely too tight. He stared at Paige with narrowed eyes for a few seconds, and with a shake of his head he said, "They won't stick around with you much longer, but I guess you already know that and simply don't care. Let's see where this damn list gets you."

He threw the door open and left Paige alone once more, though that seemed to be a common occurrence on this trip.

Kieran

Beau stormed out of the room and grabbed a six-pack of beer before heading to the hot tub downstairs. Lottie joined him a few minutes later, while everyone else continued playing the game for a while.

Paige had slammed the door shut seconds after Beau left, and Kieran was glad for it. Not because of that silly little list, but because of the fuss it was creating. Kieran knew Lottie would take offense to it, but he hadn't realized how much it would bother Beau.

Maybe he's just worried about Lottie and wants answers, Kieran thought. *Either way, Paige still gets under Beau's skin whether he admits it or not.*

That was one of the main reasons Kieran told Beau not to go out with her in the first place. Sure, she has the looks, but her personality drains the life out of you.

If only people would listen to me more.

Kieran said the same thing to Roman, giving him the not-so-subtle message of leaving her ass behind. Kieran thought she would've burned him out sooner than this, but truthfully, Kieran was just curious how long this little relationship would play out. Sensing the relief from Roman after Paige retreated to her room for the night, it appeared the relationship might have run its course.

Later, Kieran headed off to his room, when he heard muffled talking outside in the hot tub. It was past 2 a.m. at this point, and while he was more than exhausted, he also was still a little too drunk to try to sleep this off and not have a hangover tomorrow.

Kieran grabbed a glass of water before throwing on swim trunks and joining Beau and Lottie outside. When he threw open the door, their conversation halted completely; all he could hear was the rumbling water of the hot tub and the roaring crickets. They breathed a sigh of relief when they saw it was Kieran.

"No need to stop talking on my account," Kieran said, setting the glass of water on the side, putting one leg in before another as he slowly sank into the steamy water. They stared at each other awkwardly before looking back at Kieran, who rubbed some water on his face. "Come on, I know you must be talking about that list, so out with it."

Beau said, "I was just telling Lottie the conversation I had with Paige in the bedroom."

Kieran sat up, raising his eyebrows to prompt Beau to continue.

"Well, I obviously went in there to talk about the list, but she misunderstood it as something else." Kieran narrowed his eyes, and Beau said, "She kissed me."

"Wait, what?"

Beau nodded uneasily.

"Holy shit," said Kieran, "are you going to tell Roman?"

"I mean, I probably should." Beau swallowed hard.

"Are you going to tell him tonight?"

Beau had panic written in his eyes. "It's late Kieran, I don't wanna ruin his night." He stared off, looking as though he had a million thoughts running in his mind. "Besides, what if he confronts Paige while we're here. We can't possibly make this trip any worse."

Kieran shook his head. "I don't know, Beau. I think you should tell Roman sooner rather than later."

"Tell me what?" Roman said as he walked down the deck stairs to join them. Beau remained silent for a second, which angered Roman.

"Dude, what is it?" Roman slurred.

Beau took a big breath in and replied, "Paige kissed me. She said she's dating you because it distracts her from me."

Roman didn't appear to process those words as he stared at Beau, his head tilted as he tried to grasp what he had heard. Beau looked at

Lottie and Kieran, confused, before saying, "Did you hear what I said, Roman?"

Roman nodded, slight anger creeping into his features. "So, what, does that mean you will be getting back together?"

Beau looked horrified. "God, no, Roman. She took me by surprise. I had only brought her in there to talk about the list. I swear I had no idea she was going to do that, but I didn't want to keep it from you."

Roman nodded again, slowly, and if he was on the brink of tears or feeling any ounce of sadness, he blinked that away quickly. "Alright well, I'm going to go confront her now."

He swiftly turned around and almost made it to the deck before Beau rushed out of the water. He refrained from touching him, probably worried he'd start a fight. The last thing Beau needed was a broken nose coupled with a bruised eye, considering Roman was easily five inches taller and thirty pounds heavier.

"Maybe you should just leave her alone tonight, alright? No need to start up something with her right now," Beau said.

"Why the hell not? She's tried to make this trip miserable for everyone the whole time we've been here. I'm tired of her acting like this."

Lottie raised her eyebrows, and although Beau and Roman didn't see a smile break out on her face at that comment, Kieran had to stifle his laughter. He thought the same, and evidently so did Lottie.

"I'm not saying she doesn't deserve it, Roman, but why not just wait till tomorrow when our minds are a little clearer?"

Roman mulled it over for a second, and then reluctantly nodded.

Beau said, "Why don't you stay in my room, to give you some distance from her?"

Roman nodded again and headed to the room. Lottie and Kieran followed, and soon enough the house was finally quiet for the night.

Roman

In the heat of the moment, Roman wished Beau would've let him to talk to Paige. But seeing that Roman had more than a few drinks, he knew it was better to leave it for the morning. He didn't want to possibly forget her reaction when he confronted her because he had too much to drink. Roman wanted to remember all of it.

He thought about barging into the room early in the morning, but he didn't want to risk waking everyone up. Now that he was sitting in the living room, looking at her tattered notebook, he was more curious than ever to determine the meaning of the name ranking. It hadn't bothered him until this point, but he knew it bothered pretty much everyone else.

Even though Paige didn't know they'd be breaking up soon, Roman wondered if that would affect where he would rank on the list. *Would it move me from first to last?*

He wanted to ask, when Paige walked out of the room, her hair a mess as she smoothed it away from her face. She did a double take at Roman; he was sure she was confused as to why he didn't join her in bed last night.

She confirmed it by asking, "Where were you last night? You didn't come to bed."

She looked sad at this, but Roman knew it was an act, especially after what Beau admitted to him last night. He had no reason not to believe Beau. Beau didn't stir up shit if he didn't have to, especially when it came to Paige.

"I didn't want to bother you, so I just slept out here."

She narrowed her eyes. "Out on the couch?"

He shrugged. "More comfortable than you think." He could've told her about bunking with Beau, but then she might catch on, so he kept silent.

"Well, I missed having you there." She cracked a smile at him, and he wondered if it was fake, and if their whole relationship had been fake.

"I'm sure you did."

"What did you say?"

"Nothing, nevermind."

He mustered up the fakest smile he could before joining her in the kitchen. She was back to making the same breakfast as she had before, leaving Willa with barely anything to eat. That bothered him, because he knew Paige wouldn't have forgotten something like that, considering she would get more than upset when people forget her own allergies.

He decided then that he was going to have a little fun with this impending breakup. Normally, people let Paige's antics roll off their backs. But he didn't like the way she treated her friends. His parents had never liked her either, and now he could see why.

"I think you should go to the store," Roman said, simply. He leaned back on the counter and watched her grab the last carton of eggs and the last package of bacon. It would be enough for the group, but that wouldn't work for Willa, which was what he wanted to prove to her.

"Willa can't eat this, Paige. You knew about her allergies and chose to ignore it..." She opened her mouth to argue, but he continued with, "Don't even try to deny it."

Her shoulders slumped in defeat and Roman felt himself perk up with this tiny victory.

"I think it would mean a lot to her if you'd go out and get her something she can actually eat, other than the shitty burnt toast you've made," he said.

He knew he probably pissed her off with that comment, but he couldn't bring himself to care. She didn't quip anything back, surprisingly, and instead threw on a pair of shoes, grabbed car keys, and slammed the front door, which Roman knew was on purpose.

By this point, everyone else had woken up and stumbled into the kitchen.

Willa glanced at the counter and saw the eggs and bacon. She rolled her eyes. "Where's Paige?"

"I told her to go to the store and buy things you can actually eat," Roman said. Willa blushed at this and thanked Roman. He added, "Also, I wanted her to get out of the house for a bit."

"Why?" Willa asked, and Roman relayed the story to her and Hadley since they weren't at the hot tub. Their mouths were hung open by the end of it. They asked Roman how he was doing. He wanted to pretend that it didn't bother him, but he knew they'd be able to spot that.

Roman had always known that he was more in love with Paige than she was with him (if she even loved him, that is), but he didn't know the full extent until this weekend. It had been an eye-opening weekend for him in many ways.

Roman never was the type of guy to spill an ex's dirty laundry; he didn't see the point. But Paige obviously didn't get that memo. On the first date, Beau was brought up more than a few times. Now that Roman looked back on it he knew it was a glaring red flag, but he chose to ignore it.

Without dating Paige he wouldn't have met this group. Still, he wished he hadn't ignored the red flags. He hoped, at least, his new friends would side with him in the breakup.

He replied, "It hurts now, but I'll get over it. Besides, if it wasn't for her kissing Beau, I probably would've still broken up with her after this weekend anyway."

Everyone knowingly nodded and sighed, feeling relief in their agreement that Paige was more of a detriment to this friend group than anything.

"So, what? Are you just gonna confront her when she gets back?" Hadley asked.

Roman thought about it for a second, before shaking his head. "Not immediately, but I'll make sure to confront her when everybody's there." Roman knew this might be a little harsh, but he was way past caring. After all, she had made it clear that he was "just a distraction" for her, anyway.

"I think we need to get to the bottom of this list. She might open up about it after I break up with her."

Hadley shot him a look. "Do you really think that?"

He shrugged his shoulders again. "Why not?"

She clicked her tongue before responding, "Because it's Paige, and she likes to try to get on our nerves. And what better way than not telling us what it's about."

She put her hand on her hip and sighed once more, clearly fed up with Paige over the last few days.

"We can just play it by ear, right?" Roman said and as soon as he finished the last word Paige walked through the door. A confused look spread across her face as she took in the friend group standing in the living room.

"Cult much?" she whispered, but was just loud enough for everyone to hear. She grabbed the grocery items out of the bags before announcing, "I just grabbed some eggless pancake mix and yogurt, Willa. Are you fine with eating those?" She asked with a slight edge of annoyance peeking through her voice.

"Sure, that's fine, thanks," Willa replied, rolling her eyes at her, though Paige paid no attention.

"Roman, will you come help me make breakfast?"

Roman's head flickered towards the group, and he raised his eyebrows up a few times, signaling his intent to confront her. "Yeah, I guess."

"You guess? I just went to the store. It's the least you can do," she replied.

Roman exhaled, already fed up with her attitude. He just hoped he would be able to get a word in after he confronted her. He grabbed a bowl from her hands and started mixing the batter, letting silence fall over them for a couple of minutes.

The group watched as Roman mustered the courage to talk to her. Despite appearing calm and collected, Roman was anything but. His heart hammered against his chest as he poured the pancake mix onto a skillet. It was now or never, and he knew he shouldn't chicken out. It was the best chance he had to be able to break up the relationship easily.

He cleared his throat. "So?"

She whipped her head. "What?"

"You got something to tell me?" he asked, wanting to see if she'd spill. He knew she wouldn't, so when she looked at him with wide eyes and no answer, he sighed.

"You kissed Beau."

"What are you talking about?" She was careful not to glance over at Beau.

"Don't play dumb, you're not getting out of this. Beau told me."

"And you'd believe my ex-boyfriend? He's lying."

Roman could tell that Beau wanted to jump into the conversation, but held his tongue. Roman said, "I know he's not lying, Paige."

She threw him a look, one she often threw when they were arguing.

"Okay, fine. I did kiss him, but it was just one time and that's it. I was just a little drunk and got carried away." She crossed her arms against her chest and glared at Roman for doing this in front of everyone.

"You told him that you are using me as a distraction."

She scoffed and shook her head. But Roman saw from the pain in her eyes that she knew she had no argument.

"Can't get your way out of this one, can you?" he said.

"Come on, Roman. Do you really have to humiliate me in front of everyone?"

"If roles were reversed you would do this to me," he spat, growing angrier by the second.

The room fell silent for a minute. Paige had nothing to say, while Roman had too much to say, but he was trying to pick his words carefully. The rest of the group on the other hand simply sat in the living room, their heads not even facing the kitchen, but they still heard every word. Perhaps it was rude to listen in on this intense and private conversation, but Roman gave permission, and that was enough for them to justify their blatant eavesdropping.

"Don't even get me started on the elephant in the room," Roman said, each word harsher than the last.

"What the fuck are you talking about?" she yelled, still oblivious.

"Are you seriously going to play stupid?"

She palmed her face. "God, why are we still on this? It was just a stupid list, I shouldn't have even made it."

"Then why the fuck did you? That list managed to turn this whole weekend into a shitshow. You realize that, right?"

"Yes, I do," she replied, her gaze cast towards the hardwood floor.

"And you have no remorse for that?"

"I do," Paige lied.

"Oh really, you do?" Roman mimicked her voice. "I don't believe you, because if that was the case then you'd tell us what that list meant."

Paige

Paige felt their eyes burning a hole into her, but a grin formed on her face. Pleased with the mania her little list had caused.

"I've heard the murmurings about me over the past few months, how you all despise me. I planned this trip as an act of good faith, to see if you'd change your ways. But I was wrong."

The group appeared startled, not expecting that response.

Paige went on, "I purposefully fed you an egg muffin, dumped that water on your laptop, carved a hole in that canoe..." She turned to Kieran, "I wish you would've went farther in that lake."

Paige then stared at the empty coffee mugs, the ones she carefully crafted for each person. "Did you all enjoy your coffee this morning?"

Her sinister grin widened. No one offered a response, though she watched their pale faces turn green. "I wanted you all to crack, to ponder why your names appeared on the list in that order. I heard your guesses, and I must say it took everything in me to not reveal my true intent..." Paige walked around the kitchen, her face pleased as her friend's faces shriveled in pain. "That was the order I wanted to see you all die. I put enough in to kill all of you, but a little more for those on the top of the list."

As if on cue, Roman dropped first, before Willa, Hadley, Beau, and Kieran, leaving Lottie for last. Lottie, foaming at the mouth, clutched her aching stomach. Tears ran down her eyes as she stared up at Paige in terror. She collapsed on her knees, unable to withstand the growing pain any longer.

"And to think, I liked you the most," Lottie gasped, sputtering foam from her mouth.

She closed her eyes, with the last image of a laughing Paige burned into her mind.

About the Author

Bri Heron is a short story and dystopian writer that enjoys developing turbulent worlds with strong protagonists on journeys of self-acceptance and making sense of their complicated lives.

She is an Indiana Hoosier who fell in love with storytelling after discovering the intricacy of compelling world building and complex characters, pushing her to create stories of her own.

When she is not writing, she is booking her next trip, diving into the latest TV shows, checking out a new brewery with her friends, or playing with her dog.

You can find more of her writing and other links on her website at briheron.com